Thomas Jefferson

Third President of the United States

Illustrated by Kenneth Wagner

Thomas Jefferson

Third President of the United States

By Helen Albee Monsell

Aladdin Paperbacks

Aladdin Paperbacks
An imprint of Simon & Schuster
Children's Publishing Division
1230 Avenue of the Americas
New York, NY 10020
Copyright © 1939, 1953, 1962
by the Bobbs-Merrill Company, Inc.
First Aladdin Paperbacks edition, 1989
Printed in the United States of America

19 20

Library of Congress Cataloging-in-Publication Data
Monsell, Helen Albee.
Thomas Jefferson: third president of the United States/by Helen Albee Monsell. — 1st Aladdin Books ed.
p.   cm. — (The Childhood of famous Americans series)
Reprint. Originally published: Tom Jefferson: boy of colonial days. Indianapolis: Bobbs-Merrill, © 1939.
Summary: Focuses on the childhood of America's third president.
ISBN 0-689-71347-9
1. Jefferson, Thomas. 1743–1826—Childhood and youth—Juvenile literature.   2. Presidents—United States—Biography—Juvenile literature.
[1. Jefferson, Thomas, 1743–1826—Childhood and youth.   2. Presidents.]
I. Title.   II. Series.
E332.79.M57   1989   973.4'6'092—dc20
[B]   [92]   89-37841   CIP   AC

To Elizabeth Duval
Loyal Virginian

Illustrations

Contents

CHILDHOOD
OF FAMOUS
AMERICANS
®

★ Thomas Jefferson

Third President of the United States

At Tuckahoe

It was a warm spring morning in 1748. Two children were running down the steep hill at Tuckahoe. Down! Down!

Tom couldn't have stopped if he'd wanted to. He would have lost his balance and tumbled the rest of the way. He didn't want to stop, though. The wind was in his hair. The sun was on his back. Down, down, down! This was fun!

He was out of breath when he reached the bottom of the hill. He was only five years old. His sister Jane was eight, and she was breathless too. They drooped down on the ground to rest.

"You would have lost your sunbonnet if it

hadn't been sewed on," Tom told his sister. "I am glad I don't have to wear a sunbonnet sewed onto my head whenever I go out."

"Girls have to be very careful," said Jane. "You are just a boy. Nobody cares whether boys get freckles or not."

"I am glad of that." Tom knew there were plenty of freckles on his nose and forehead.

Buttercups grew all around them. He picked one and twirled it under his sister's chin.

"Stop it!" Jane laughed. "You are tickling me."

"I just wanted to see if you liked butter."

"How about yourself?" Jane picked another buttercup and reached toward him.

Tom rolled out of the way quickly. "You don't need to try it on me. You already know I like it. I want piles of butter on my spoon bread and hot biscuit and corncakes and *everything*!"

Jane dropped her buttercup. It fell into a patch of clover.

"Oh, look! Let's find a four-leaf clover. We can get Mother to press it in a book for us and it will bring us all sorts of good luck."

"I would like to look for a four-leaf clover, too, but I'm thirsty," said Tom.

"So am I. There is a spring over yonder underneath that poplar tree."

They left the clover patch. They ran over to the poplar tree. Jane stood on tiptoe to reach the lowest branch. She pulled off some big leaves.

"I am going to make us some leaf cups."

"I'd like to make one, too," Tom said.

"All right. Find us some thorns first."

It didn't take Tom long to find the thorns. There were some long, sharp ones on the bushes right back of the poplar tree. It wasn't easy, though, to break them off. He got almost as many scratches as he did thorns.

Finally he held up a very small handful. "Is this enough?" he called anxiously.

"That is plenty. We aren't making cups for the whole plantation."

Tom ran back to her. "Now, show me."

Jane folded a big poplar leaf into a cup shape. She fastened the corners with thorns.

"Now I'll make one by myself," said Tom.

"All right. It never does take you long to learn how to do things."

As soon as the cups were ready they dipped them down into the spring. The water leaked out at the corners. It was hard work to drink without spilling it all over themselves. They had to dip their cups again and again.

"It certainly is good water," said Tom.

"You just think that now because you are so thirsty."

"Maybe so."

"Or because you made your own cup."

"Maybe so," said Tom again. Then he grinned. "Come on. I'll race you back up to the house."

14

The hill was too steep for fast racing. It wasn't long before they had slowed down to a walk. Both were puffing when they reached the big plantation house. They were glad to drop down to rest on the stone steps to the big porch.

They could look down the hill toward the spring. Beyond the spring they could see the lowlands, where tobacco and corn were growing. Beyond the lowlands they could see the James River. It was a muddy red color. It was the only river Tom could remember.

He thought all rivers ran through lowland fields with high hills close by. Sometimes there would be houses on the hills, where people lived. More often there would be woods. He was sure that wherever there was a river there must be hills, too.

"Of course not," said Jane. "It is different everywhere you go. Down around Williamsburg, the land is flat. The hills around our own home are much higher than they are here."

Tom was puzzled. He turned and looked at the big house behind him.

"Isn't this our own home?" he asked.

Jane shook her head. "This is Tuckahoe. Tuckahoe is Tom Randolph's home."

"Why isn't it our home, too? We live here, don't we?"

"We've been here for a long time," Jane said, "but we don't live here. Our own home is at Shadwell."

"Then why do we stay here? Do you know?"

"Of course I know. Father explained it to me once. He said he and Tom Randolph's father were old friends. They had always helped each other in every way they could. Before Mr. Randolph died, he asked Father to take care of Tuckahoe for Tom.

"Now Shadwell is a long way from Tuckahoe.

The roads are very bad. It takes two days and sometimes more to get from one place to the other. Father said he couldn't stay in Shadwell and look out for things here. He had to move his family down, so he could stay here."

"I remember, now," said Tom. "It is the very first thing I do remember. I remember when we moved here."

"You can't," Jane told him. "You were such a little boy. You were only two years old."

"I can remember, just the same."

"Do you remember anything about what Shadwell looked like?"

Tom shook his head. "No. I can't remember anything about that."

"Do you remember the road down here, through the woods, with all the wild grapevines, and how once we saw a bear?"

"No. I can't remember that."

"What *do* you remember?"

"I remember, when we started, somebody handed me up to one of the servants on horseback. I don't remember which servant it was, but I sat on a pillow, in front of him."

Jane laughed. "No wonder you remember that! I remember it, too. You were so proud sitting up there on the horse, like a man, instead of being in the coach with Mother and the nurse, like a baby."

"When we go back to Shadwell, I'll be riding my own horse," said Tom.

"I wouldn't be a bit surprised," said Jane.

HOW TO MAKE DINNERTIME COME

There were a good many houses at Tuckahoe. First, of course, there was the big house. It looked like a mother hen with all her baby chicks clustered around her.

Then there was the kitchen. Tom thought that

18

was a very important place. The kitchen was a little house, all by itself, with a path that led to the dining-room door. Then there was the office where Father kept all his letters and papers. There were the laundry and the smokehouse, the stable and the coach house.

There was another building close by the big house. It was used for a schoolhouse. It was a very small building, with only one room, but a big schoolhouse was not necessary with only two or three children in the school.

Tom's sisters didn't go to school except for a very short time. They went long enough to learn to read, write, and do a very little arithmetic. That was all a girl was supposed to learn in school in 1748. It wasn't necessary for her to learn how to spell any but the very easiest words. Girls simply didn't have to bother about things like that.

"You have a mighty easy time of it," Tom

Randolph told Jane. "Just sitting around playing with your doll babies while we poor boys are
shut up in that old schoolhouse!"

"I should say we don't have an easy time!"
Jane was indignant. "*You* don't have to learn all
about spinning and weaving! Mother was teaching me to knit and sew long before you began
your *a-b-c's*!"

"Girl things like that are easy."

"Try them."

"Not me!"

"Besides, when school is over for the day, *you*
can go off hunting or swimming or do whatever
you want to do. *I* have to practice on the spinet
for hours and hours. When the servants are
sick I must go with Mother to learn how to take
care of them. Then I must learn how to keep
house. Why, I work twice as long and hard as
you boys ever do!"

Tom Randolph laughed, but Tom Jefferson

certainly felt sorry for his sister if she had to work any harder than he did. Now that he was five he had to stay in the schoolhouse all morning from breakfast to dinnertime.

It wouldn't have been so bad if the schoolmaster had taught him how to *do* things or how to *make* them. He didn't. All he wanted Tom to do was to *learn* things. He never explained why or what for. All he did was to hear Tom "say his lessons." He never asked, "Do you understand?" That didn't seem to make any difference.

Tom learned to say his *a-b-c's*. He could say them with his eyes shut. He could say them from *a* to *z* without stopping. Nobody explained, though, that they would help him to read.

On Sunday there was no school. He could forget his *a-b-c's* for a little while.

There was something else now, though, to be learned by heart. Jane was teaching him the Lord's Prayer.

Tom sat on a stool by the fireplace in his mother's room. Through the window, he could see the sunlight dancing on the grass. Two dogs were chasing each other around the yard. Oh, how he wanted to be outdoors! But he must learn the prayer first.

" 'Forgive us our trespasses,' " said Jane.

" 'Forgive us our trespasses,' " Tom repeated.

Jane didn't explain what the long words meant. How could she? Nobody had ever explained them to Jane.

Tom didn't even understand, exactly, what a prayer was. Nobody explained to him that a boy who prayed was really talking with God. No one explained how, in his prayers, he could thank God for the beautiful world in which he lived, and for his father and mother, who were taking care of him.

"A good little boy must learn to say his prayers." That was all Tom knew. Somehow,

though, he thought that, if you could say your prayers, you could make anything happen that you wanted to happen. He thought it was like knowing a witch's spell.

" 'For Thine is the kingdom,' " said Jane.

" 'For Thine is the kingdom,' " Tom recited after her.

"Now let's see if you can say it all the way through without a mistake."

Tom closed his eyes tight. "Our Father—" he began.

He said it all the way through without a mistake. He said it as fast as he could.

"Good!" said Jane.

Tom had learned his prayer. Now he could go outdoors, in the sunlight. He could run down to the kitchen, with the two dogs at his heels, to see if dinner was nearly ready.

It was hard to go back to school again Monday morning. The teacher in the little schoolhouse was a man. He was called a tutor. Tom had decided his very first day in school that tutors didn't believe in spoiling little boys.

"I wonder what he will want me to learn today," thought Tom. "I am through with those old *a-b-c*'s anyway."

He soon found out that he wasn't. The tutor had made him a copy of the whole alphabet.

"Now that you can say your letters you must learn to write them. This is *a*. Write *a*."

Tom made a wobbly *a*.

"This is *b*. Write *b*."

Tom tried and tried, until he could make a nice fat *b*.

It was very slow work, and very uninteresting. Tom's hand grew tired. He wrote *a* and *b* again and again. His hand grew *very* tired.

"Now write *ab*."

It seemed to him that dinnertime was mighty slow coming. Maybe the fire had gone out in the kitchen! Maybe the dogs had stolen the big roast of beef that he had seen on the kitchen table that morning! Maybe dinnertime never would come!

"*A-b, ab.*" Tom wrote it again.

Then, suddenly, he remembered something. He could say his prayers, now. He could use the prayer like a witch's spell. He could make dinnertime come.

The tutor was hearing Tom Randolph's lessons. He didn't notice when Tom Jefferson quietly slipped out the door of the schoolroom.

Tom went around to the corner of the building farthest away from the house. He closed his eyes tight.

"Our Father who art in Heaven," said Tom.

He said the whole prayer through. He said it as fast as he could. He said it without a mistake.

Then he slipped back into the schoolroom. He began to write again.

Now he was happy. He had said his prayer. He was certain that it would make dinnertime come right away.

"*A-b*," wrote Tom.

"*Ding-dong!*" went the dinner bell.

Dinnertime had come. Lessons were over for the day—and Tom thought he had made it happen all by himself!

FATHER COMES BACK

The days were growing colder. There was a big fire in the fireplace in Mother's room. Tom liked to watch it blaze and listen to it crackle. He liked to watch Mother knitting in front of the fire. He liked to watch Jane playing with Baby Martha. They stayed close enough to the blaze to keep warm, but far enough away to keep any flying sparks from burning them.

Tom missed Father. When a boy is six years

old, even two or three days seem like a long time. Father had been away for weeks. It seemed to Tom as if he had been away for years.

"I wish Father would come home," said Tom.

Mother wished he would come, too, but she wouldn't let the children see that she was worried. "I'm sure he will get back soon," she said.

"Tonight?"

"Well, maybe not tonight."

"Tomorrow, then?"

"Maybe, or maybe next week."

"He has been gone for weeks and weeks, already, Mother!"

Jane looked up. "You have to be away for weeks and weeks when you are doing important work for your king and country, the way Father is," she told Tom.

"What is Father doing? Is he fighting the Indians?"

Mother shook her head. "Fighting the Indians

isn't the only way to help your country," she told him.

"Then what *is* Father doing?"

"The first people who came to Virginia," said Mother, "built their homes on the banks of the big rivers, not so many miles from the ocean. The first settlers in North Carolina did the same thing. Now, people are moving west. They are building their homes all the way back to the mountains. No map has ever been made of this part of the country. These people can't tell whether they are living in Virginia or in North Carolina. The line between the two has never been run any farther than Peter's Creek.

"Your father and Mr. Fry have gone to Peter's Creek. They were going to meet some men from North Carolina there. Then they were going to run the line all the way over the mountains."

"There are rattlesnakes in the mountains!" said Tom.

"Yes," said Mother.

"There are wild bears and wolves!"

"Yes," agreed Mother.

"Oh," said Tom, "I *do* wish Father would come back!"

The next day and the next, it rained. They weren't just short little showers, with the sun peeping out between. All day long it rained and rained and rained.

On the afternoon of the second day, Tom stood staring out the window. His nose was pressed flat against the glass.

He looked down the long lane in front of the house. There were big cedar trees on each side of the lane. The cedar trees were heavy with rain.

"Mother!" called Tom. "Someone is coming. Oh! I do believe it is Father!"

How excited everybody was! The dogs ran barking down the lane to meet him. The servants came running from the kitchen and the stables.

Tom ran out into the rain, too. Mother and the girls stood in the doorway, waiting.

The legs of Father's horse were caked with mud. Father himself was pretty well covered with mud. He looked very tired and thin.

He was back — and he was safe. Mother looked very happy.

Dinner was over long ago. Father hadn't stopped anywhere to eat, though, because he was so anxious to get home. The fire in the kitchen was out, but there was cold roast beef left over from dinner. There was also plenty of cold corn bread.

"Roast beef and corn bread," said Father. "What a feast!"

It didn't seem much like a feast to the children, though.

"Didn't you have roast beef while you were gone?" asked Jane.

"Not in the mountains," said Father. "Deer

and bear meat mostly—if we could find any. Sometimes there would be days when we couldn't scare up even a squirrel. Sometimes, when we had meat, it rained so hard we couldn't build a fire to cook it."

"So you didn't have anything but cold bread for dinner!" said Tom.

"I'd have been mighty thankful for a piece of cold bread," said Father, "but the bread gave out weeks ago."

"Then why didn't you come back?"

"I had started out to run the line all the way over the mountains."

Outside, the rain was pouring down. They heard it beating on the roof. Father listened.

"It's been a long time since I've been inside a house when it rained."

"Where did you sleep?" asked Jane.

"On the ground, mostly. Sometimes that wasn't safe, because the rain would put the fire

out, and there were too many wolves around. Once I slept in a hollow tree."

Jane shivered. Little Martha shivered, too.

"But you ran the line all the way across the mountains, didn't you Father?" asked Tom.

"Yes," said Father. He leaned back in his chair and smiled.

He had been on a long and dangerous journey. He was very weary, but he had done what he started out to do. He was satisfied.

Somehow, Tom knew exactly how he felt.

Back Home

THE ROAD wound through the pine woods. It was such a narrow road a man could stand in the middle and almost touch the trees on each side. It was a very rough road, too. It was filled with holes and bumps and roots of trees and little pools of water.

Squirrels ran up and down the trees. There was a mockingbird singing close by. People came along this road so seldom that the animals and birds felt it was all their own.

Suddenly one of the squirrels stopped short. His head was straight down. His bushy tail was straight up. He cocked his head to one side and

listened. The mockingbird stopped singing. Something was coming down the road—something strange to bird and animal.

The mockingbird flew away. The squirrels whisked into their holes. One of them, braver than the others, peeped out. He had never seen so many people!

Peter Jefferson had finished his work at Tuckahoe. He was moving his family back to their home at Shadwell.

He rode through the woods on his big horse. Behind him came Tom. Tom was nine years old now. Some people said his hair was sandy-colored. Some people called it red. There were freckles across his nose. He wore a deerskin hunting jacket, and he rode his own horse.

Behind Tom came the coach. It was pulled by four tugging horses. Mother and the girls rode in the coach.

There were four girls now. Jane and Mary

were older than Tom. Martha and Elizabeth were younger.

Behind the coach came the servants with the extra horses. These horses carried big packs. There was food for the horses, and food for the people, too, because dinnertime might come when they were miles away from any house.

Then there were the children's clothes and all the new things Mother was taking back for the home at Shadwell.

No wonder the squirrels were surprised. They hadn't seen so many people and horses and packs in their woods for days and days.

Where the road was wide enough, Tom rode beside the coach. That was the way young men did when they wanted to talk with the young ladies inside. Of course, he wasn't a young man, yet, but there was no harm in practicing.

Jane sat at the coach window holding Martha. She was telling Martha about Shadwell.

"It isn't nearly so big a place as Tuckahoe," she said.

"It is home, though," said Tom.

"What does it look like?" asked Martha.

"It is a frame house with two brick chimneys. Downstairs, there are four rooms and a hall. Upstairs, there are some very small bedrooms."

"There are hills all around, and, away off, you can see the mountains," said Tom, with pride. "Father told me so."

"What is a mountain?" asked Martha.

Jane laughed. "The questions that child can ask! You tell her, Tom."

Tom didn't laugh. He knew how Martha felt, because he liked to ask questions too.

He himself hadn't seen a mountain since he was two years old.

"A mountain is like a big hill," he said, "only ever so much bigger. Isn't that right, Jane?"

Jane nodded her head. Of course, she hadn't

been so very big when they left Shadwell but she remembered the mountains.

"Is a mountain as big as two hills, Tom?" persisted Martha.

Tom didn't know the answer to that. He looked at Jane again. Jane looked at Mother.

"A very, very big hill is the same thing as a very, very little mountain," said Mother.

"Oh!"

"Father owns a little mountain," said Jane. "I remember it. You can see it from the window at Shadwell."

"My," thought Tom, "how nice to have a mountain right in your own family!"

He made up his mind to climb their own mountain as soon as he could.

They were leaving the pine woods behind them now. They climbed a long, low hill.

There were fields in front of them. In the middle of the fields was a small house. It was a frame house with two brick chimneys. It was a story and a half high.

"Yonder is Shadwell," said Father. "We are home at last."

Jane was delighted. "I do remember it!" she cried. "It looks just the way I thought it would."

Tom hardly looked at the house. Away in the distance he saw the little mountain. It wasn't just a hill. Neither was it such a big mountain that it made you afraid. It was just the right size. Already, it seemed to Tom that he and the little mountain belonged to each other.

GETTING USED TO HOME

The next few days were the most exciting that Tom had ever known. There were so many new things to see and to do and to find out.

Of course, not everything was really new. He had been born here in Shadwell.

"You learned to walk right there in Mother's room," Jane told him, "and to climb. You could climb up to the top of that chest of drawers faster than a squirrel up a walnut tree. You were a regular little monkey. It used to take Mammy and Mother and me, all three of us, to keep up with you."

"I reckon I had fun here all right, only I just can't remember it at all. I feel as if everything is brand new."

"Well, a whole lot of it is. The house wasn't even finished when we moved to Tuckahoe. Don't you remember how often Father had to come back to make sure the workmen were doing things the way he wanted them done?"

"Mother never came back, though."

"She couldn't. It was too far. That is why she is so excited now. Lots of things are as new to her as they are to you. She has been going around all day looking and admiring and deciding what she is going to change. Mother has right positive ideas, you know."

Tom laughed. He knew! A good many of her ideas were about what boys should and shouldn't do. Maybe he'd better slip away while she was still measuring that corner cupboard.

"Why don't you go out to the kitchen?" Jane suggested. Liza Ann hasn't had a chance to get a good look at you yet."

"Who is Liza Ann?"

"She is our cook. Goodness, Tom! Don't let her know you have forgotten her. Her feelings would be so hurt she'd probably put salt into the pudding instead of sugar, while she was mourning about your not remembering her."

"I'll be careful," said Tom.

"You had better go down to the stables, too. The men there will like to have you say 'hello,' and you can see our fine horses."

"I always like it when you tell me I *ought*

to do something I already *want* to do. It makes me feel so comfortable."

"Get along with you!" Jane shook her apron at him as if he were a chicken. "Shoo! You are keeping me from my work."

Tom slipped through the door. He stood a minute to drink in the fresh crisp spring air. It made him feel as frisky as a rabbit.

"I'll go to the kitchen first," he decided. "If Liza Ann is anything like the cook down at Tuckahoe she'll probably want to fix me a snack. Of course, I don't need it right now, so soon after breakfast. It is always a good idea, though, to have one in my pocket in case I get hungry before dinner."

Liza Ann was delighted to see him. Maybe he didn't remember her, but she remembered him all right. "Good lands!" she cried. "How you have grown!"

The maids and the houseboy were in the

kitchen. They were finishing their breakfast. They all commented on how he had grown.

Tom was glad to get away from them and run down to the stables. Before he left, Liza Ann slipped a snack into his hand.

"We mustn't let you get hungry the first day you are here," she told him.

Down in the stables an old man was polishing some harness. "Good lands!" he cried when he saw Tom. "How you've grown!"

Tom wanted to say "Good lands!" himself. Had everyone expected him to keep on being a two-year-old baby all his life? For a moment he felt downright cross. Then he looked up. Across the stable yard, beyond the fields, beyond the woods, he saw the little mountain. He was sure its green trees were waving to him. He couldn't look at it and stay cross for very long.

"Has the little mountain grown too, while I've been away?" he asked.

The old man laughed. "I reckon that little mountain — she just stays put."

"I am glad of that," thought Tom. He didn't understand why, exactly. He knew he would never want to "stay put" himself. He wanted to go to new places and see new things. It would be good to know, though, that the little mountain would always be there waiting, whenever he came back.

Is It Enough?

IT SEEMED to Tom that the days at Shadwell were never long enough to do all the things that he wanted to do.

He would ride over the farm with his father nearly every day. It was a very big farm. They called it a plantation. Much of it was covered with thick woods. There were fields of grass for the sheep and the cows. There were fields of wheat and fields of corn. Biggest of all, though, were the vast fields of tobacco.

Tobacco was a very important product to the farmers in Virginia when Tom was a boy. They used it in place of money. A turkey cost forty pounds of tobacco. A bushel of flour cost forty-five pounds. Even the minister's salary was paid in tobacco.

The tobacco grew in large fields. When the leaves were ripe, the plants were cut. They were hung in barns until they were dried. The dried leaves were packed in big barrels, called hogsheads. There would be almost a thousand pounds of tobacco in one hogshead.

The hogsheads of tobacco were sent to England in big boats. These big boats couldn't come all the way up the river to Shadwell. The river was too narrow and shallow. The big boats could come only as far as Richmond, so Father had to send his tobacco on down the river to Richmond.

The Rivanna River was a very small river. Father had to use a very small boat. Really it wasn't a boat at all. It was made of canoes, fastened together like a raft.

"Today," said Father, "we shall load tobacco. It is time to get it down to Richmond."

Their horses were waiting for them. As soon as breakfast was over, Tom and his father rode down to the river.

Already the men were rolling the big hogsheads of tobacco down to the riverbank. It was hard work, but they were strong men. They pushed and they tugged until their backs were wet and shiny. They rolled the hogsheads just down to the riverbank.

Now, if they rolled any farther, the hogsheads would fall into the river. They must be made to stand up on one end.

Since each hogshead weighed nearly a thousand pounds, it wasn't easy to stand them up on end. The men pushed and tugged.

"Here!" said Father. He jumped down from his horse.

He stood between two hogsheads and put one hand on the head of each.

"Now!"

He began to pull. The muscles stood out in his arms. He pulled on both hogsheads until they stood up straight on end.

"Hurrah!" Tom cheered loudly. He was sure that never had there been anyone quite so strong as Father.

THE SHED CAME DOWN

After the tobacco was loaded, Tom and his father rode back up the hill. Tom was still excited. He wondered if he could ever grow to be as strong as Father.

Father wasn't excited at all. He had already started to think of something else.

"Look at that shed," he told Tom.

Tom looked. They were riding by one of the

49

old fields on the farm. Once it had been planted in tobacco. Now it wasn't used at all. Weeds had overgrown the whole field. There were goldenrod and wild onions and Queen Anne's lace. Blackberry bushes grew thick along the edge of the field.

In the middle of the field was an old shed. It had been a good place to store things when the men were working the tobacco. Now it was empty. Its door was off the hinges. Its roof was sagging. It looked as if it were about to fall in.

"It is an eyesore," said Mr. Jefferson, "and it is a good place for rats and other varmints. As soon as we've finished dinner I am going to bring some men to pull it down."

"How can you pull a house down?" asked Tom.

"It won't be too hard. We'll fasten ropes to the roof. Then if two or three men give them a good hard pull I expect it will come down without any trouble."

When Father made up his mind to do a thing, he never wasted any time over it. As soon as dinner was over, he called three of the men who had been helping load the tobacco. He sent them to the storehouse for long coils of rope. Then they went out to the old field. He fastened the ropes to the roof of the shed. He gave the ends of the rope to the three men.

"Pull!" he said. "Pull hard!"

The men pulled. They pulled with all their strength. Nothing happened.

"Rest a minute," said Mr. Jefferson. "Then try it again."

They tried again. " 'Tisn't a bit of use," said the biggest man. "You can't expect three men to pull a whole house down by themselves."

"It is just a small shed," said Father. "Try it again."

No matter how hard they tried, the shed still stood there.

"I reckon we'll have to get a hammer and knock it down a plank at a time," one man said.

"Wait a minute," said Mr. Jefferson. "I'll try it myself."

He jumped down from his horse, went to the shed, and picked up the ends of two of the ropes. He put them over his back and pulled.

The old shed creaked and groaned. He pulled harder still. Tom heard something crack. His father kept on pulling.

Tom could see his father's muscles knot. Big beads of sweat stood on his forehead. He pulled harder and harder. Then there was another crack. The walls were caving in!

Tom began to shout. There arose a big cloud of dust. The shed had fallen!

Father dropped the rope. He dusted his hands and wiped his forehead.

"You see," he told the men quietly. "It *could* be done. Now you take the ropes back to the

storehouse and get back to your work at the wharf. I'll send the carpenter over here in the morning to get the nails. We can use them again."

He mounted his horse again. "We'll ride down to the mill next, Tom."

Tom rode along by his father. He looked at his broad shoulders. How wonderful it must be to be able to up-end two big hogsheads of tobacco and pull a house down all by yourself!

"Do you suppose," he asked, "that I shall ever be as strong as you are?"

His father laughed. "It is more than likely. We Jeffersons usually have plenty of muscle."

Then he grew serious. "But that isn't enough, son. Oh, I know that it is a fine thing to have a strong healthy body. You have one now and I hope you will always keep it that way.

"Just to be strong isn't enough, though. You must have a trained mind in that strong body of yours."

"I can read," said Tom, "and I can write. I know some arithmetic, too."

"That is all that many boys learn," said Father. "That is all the schooling I had, myself. It isn't enough.

"All my life I have had to study, by myself, to make up what I missed. I don't want you to miss it. You must go back to school."

Tom hadn't been at Shadwell very long. He wasn't sure he wanted to go away again so soon.

There was the little mountain. He wanted to climb that again and again, until he knew all the little paths the animals had made. He wanted to climb up to the very top.

The little mountain could wait, though. It had been there before he came. It would be there when he got back.

"A trained mind in a strong body." Father was right. That was very important.

Indians

Tom was sitting in the big hall by the door. He was cleaning his gun. When Mrs. Jefferson wanted fresh meat she couldn't send someone to the store to buy it. Someone had to go to the woods to shoot it. Tom was ten years old now. He was getting ready to go hunting with his father early the next morning.

Suddenly he heard someone calling him. "Mister Tom! Mister Tom!" It was his own servant.

Caesar came running up the path from the river. He came running across the yard. "Mister Tom!" he called. "The Indians are here!"

Tom put his gun down in a hurry. "I'm coming," he called to Caesar.

"Before you finish cleaning your gun, son?" asked Father.

Tom looked sheepish. He knew better, indeed, than to leave before he finished his work.

"I mean—I'm coming as soon as I finish this," he said. He picked up his gun again.

"Do you think it is safe for Tom to go down to the Indian camp?" asked his mother.

"I think so," said Father. "Chief Ontassete is my friend. He knows he can trust me. I know I can trust him. My son will be quite welcome to sit by his campfires."

"I heard a man say once," Tom told him, "that the only good Indian is a dead Indian. That isn't so, is it, Father?"

Father shook his head. "Indians are like everyone else. If you treat them well, they'll treat you well. The white men haven't treated

them well, though. We have taken their land. We have driven away their game from the forests. We are driving the Indians themselves, back over the mountains. No wonder they want to fight back. I am afraid that someday we are going to have a terrible Indian war."

"Chief Ontassete won't fight, will he?"

"Not now. His tribe is too weak. He feels that the best way to help his people now is to be friends with the white man."

"There!" Tom had finished cleaning his gun. He hung it up where the babies couldn't reach it. "Now I am ready, Caesar."

The two boys ran across the yard. They ran down the path toward the river.

He was glad the Indians trusted his father so much that they would camp on his land. He was glad that he would be welcome to sit with them by their campfires.

Caesar wasn't sure he wanted to go right into

the Indian camp. A person couldn't always tell when the Indians were going to change their minds about being friendly, but, if Mister Tom was going, Caesar was going too.

Mister Tom was most certainly going. No one could keep him away.

"Are there many of them?" Tom asked Caesar.

Caesar nodded. "I reckon it's the whole tribe," he said.

"Where are they going?"

"I don't know. It must be somewhere special, 'cause the chief's all dressed up. Injuns talk so funny, no one can understand what they say, though."

"They talk the Indian language," said Tom, "the way we talk English. I wonder if all Indians use the same language. You know, it would be fun to find out. I could write down certain words in a notebook—tree, bird, fire, and things like that. Then I could ask all the different kinds

59

of Indians I see what their word for each of them is."

It was a good idea. Right now there was no more time to think about it, but he tucked it away in his mind.

They hurried on until they had almost reached the river.

"There they are!" cried Caesar.

There they were, indeed. The Indians were making their camp. The women were building the fires and getting supper ready. Children and dogs seemed to be everywhere. They bumped into their mothers. They knocked over the big kettles. They almost tumbled into the fires.

Tom went from one fire to another. The Indian women smiled at him. The children stared at him with big serious eyes. The Indian men greeted Tom in their own language.

Now the kettles were hung over the fires. The stew began to bubble. It smelled very good, but Tom and Caesar weren't sure they wanted any. They weren't used to the Indians' food. The Indian women were kind, but they couldn't tell the boys what was in the pots. Tom decided he'd rather eat supper in his own home.

Chief Ontassete had been to see Father. He was just leaving when Tom got back to the house.

What a fine-looking man he was! He was tall and straight. He looked very serious.

"Where are Ontassete and his people going?" Tom asked Father.

"Ontassete," said Father, "is telling his people good-by tonight. He is going down to Williamsburg. Then he will go across the ocean to London. He is going to try to explain to the King and his friends what the Indians need."

London seemed a long, long way off, even to him, and he was a white boy. He had cousins in London. His mother had been born there. How much farther away it must seem to Ontassete! He would be alone, without friends, in a strange land.

"Why is he going?"

"He is a chief," said Father, "and a chief must do whatever he can to help his people."

"Oh!" said Tom.

He had always thought it would be fun to be a chief because a chief could do what he pleased.

He couldn't. Now Tom understood that no matter how hard and unpleasant it was, a chief must do whatever he could for his people.

Mother came to the door. "Do come in to supper, Mr. Jefferson," she said to Father. "I declare, I don't know which one of you gets more excited over the Indians—you or Tom."

THE NIGHT OF THE FULL MOON

As soon as supper was over, Tom hurried back to the Indian camp. Their supper was over, too, but the Indians still sat around their fires. The moon was rising over the tops of the trees. It was a full moon. The whole camp was bright with golden moonlight.

One of the Indians rose from his place by the fire. It was Ontassete. He stepped up on a big, flat rock and held out his arms. The whole camp grew very still. Ontassete began to speak.

It was plain to see that he was praying to the Great Spirit. Tom couldn't understand the words, but all his life he remembered the fine old Indian as he stood there, praying for his people.

Ontassete was going across the Great Water to a strange country. Maybe he would die there, alone and far away, but no matter what happened, he must do what he could for his people. He was their chief.

Schoolboys Together

"*CLAPPETY-CLAP!*" went Mr. Jefferson's horse over the rocky road.

"*Clappety-clap!*" went Tom's horse, too.

"*Clappety-clap!*" went the servant's horse, coming along behind them.

Tom was on his way to school again.

There were no public schools in Virginia. The only boys who could get an education were those whose fathers could pay somebody to teach them. There never had been any public schools. It was very hard to get a good teacher.

Some of Father's friends sent their sons all the way to England to school. The boys would be

young men before they could ever come home again. Father didn't want Tom to be away that long. Tom didn't want to be away from the family and home that long, either.

There was a minister who lived down in Goochland County. His name was William Douglass. He had some extra rooms in his house. He could take five or ten boys to live with him. He could teach them in the room where he wrote his sermons. They could get back home in one or two days. That would be fine!

Tom was on his way to school at Mr. Douglass' home now.

"Yonder is the church," said Father, "and yonder is Mr. Douglass' home. Look! The boys are out playing in the yard."

Tom looked. A strange, shivery feeling ran down his back.

Tom Randolph, at Tuckahoe, had been just enough older than Tom Jefferson to make him

feel that he was only a little boy. Jane and his other sisters were very nice, but, of course, they were just girls. Tom had never had any boys his own age to play with, before. It made him excited, and a little frightened.

Father and Tom rode up to the gate. They waited while the servant got down from his horse to open it. They rode into the yard and got down from their horses.

The boys stopped playing. They stood and looked at Tom. He stood and looked at them. He felt himself growing very red. He knew he was skinny. He knew he had red hair. He knew he had freckles on his face. He felt as if the boys were counting every freckle.

Mr. Douglass came to the door. He called the boys by name. There were John, David, Peter, James, and Daniel. And there were others whose names Tom couldn't even remember. He wasn't sure which was which.

"These will be your son's schoolmates," Mr. Douglass said to Father.

The boys made stiff little bows, as if they were grown men. Then Mr. Douglass and Father went inside. The servant took the horses around to the stable. Tom was left alone with the boys.

Tom looked at the boys. They looked at Tom.

"Say," one of them asked, "can you swim?"

Tom nodded his head yes.

"It's too cold to go swimming," the boy called John said. "Can you shoot?"

Tom nodded his head again. They didn't have their guns, so they couldn't try him on that.

"Let's go over in the woods," said Daniel. "Maybe we can find some nuts."

The boys went across the road into the woods. There were plenty of briars and underbrush, but they didn't mind that. They wore stout boots. They wore trousers and hunting jackets made of tough deerskin. The briars couldn't hurt them.

"I smell persimmons," said Tom.

The boys stopped short. They looked all around. Sure enough, there was a persimmon tree, right ahead of them.

James picked up a persimmon. It was round and smooth and purple-orange.

"Here," he said, "this first one is yours, because you found the tree."

Tom laughed. They must think he was a baby, not to know a green persimmon when he saw one. They wanted to make him bite it.

Tom knew that a ripe persimmon was wrinkled and squashy-soft. He knew that green persimmons, which looked so smooth and fine, were bitter enough to turn one's mouth inside out.

If he didn't take the green persimmon, the boys might think he was afraid—and they might want to fight. He wasn't afraid to fight, but it would be a silly thing to do.

He remembered something which his Father

used to say. "Always take things by the smooth handle."

Tom looked up at the tree. There was one persimmon left at the very tiptop.

"Yonder is my persimmon," said Tom.

He picked up a stick. He aimed it very carefully. He threw it as hard as he could. It knocked the persimmon from the tiptop branch.

"Good!" cried Dan.

Tom picked up his persimmon. It was round and smooth and purple-orange. He knew it was very green.

He handed it to James. "If you will eat my persimmon, I'll eat yours," he said.

Everybody laughed. They liked a good joke.

Suddenly Tom felt happy. He didn't care if he was skinny. He didn't care if he did have freckles and red hair. He knew the boys didn't care about those things, either. They were all going to be good friends.

B-r-r, but it was cold! Tom poked his nose out carefully from beneath the blankets. The cold seemed to snap at it.

The winter sun was lazy. The boys were always up before it came peeping over the trees. This morning, though, there was a strange whiteness outside.

Tom jumped up and ran to the window. He pulled the bedclothes after him.

The boy in bed with him was awake in a hurry, then. "Hey, there!" he called. "Bring back that blanket!"

"It's snowing!" cried Tom.

That awakened the other boys in the room. They came running to the window. They didn't stay there long. It was too cold for that.

They hustled into their clothes as quickly as possible. Then they ran down the narrow stairs and tumbled into the dining room.

There was a roaring fire in the big fireplace. Tom didn't expect to get warm all over at the same time. When he stood with his face to the fire, his cheeks grew rosy-red and his toes tingled, but shivers still ran down his back. When he turned around, though, his back almost scorched, but his face and nose felt as if he had rubbed them with an icicle. He was glad when breakfast was brought in. He knew that he could then get warm from the inside out.

At home, Tom had hot corn bread for breakfast, with big slices of pink ham. Mr. Douglass and his wife came from Scotland. They had oatmeal for breakfast. Tom thought it tasted very queer, but it was hot!

As soon as breakfast was over, the boys ran outdoors. My, but the snow was deep! It must have been snowing all night. In some places it came up nearly to Tom's knees.

"Watch out!" called John. He came running

toward Tom with a big handful of snow. "I'm going to wash your face!"

"Come on!" cried Tom. He scooped up a handful of snow, too.

Such tumbling and scuffling! Both faces got washed with plenty of snow.

"Quit fooling around!" Dan begged them. "Let's build a snow fort. Then we'll play Indians and Settlers."

"I want Tom on my side," said John.

He knew Tom had strong arms. He knew he had a good aim. When Tom threw a snowball, it landed just where he meant it to land.

"I'm going to be an Indian," said Tom. "I like the Indians."

"Most folks say they are tricky and cruel. They'll scalp you if they get the chance."

"They'll treat you right if you treat them right," said Tom. He believed that all his life. He tried to help the Indians whenever he could.

"Stop arguing and get to work," Dan told them. "We haven't much time."

Dan was right. They didn't have much time. Before the walls of the snow fort were waist high, Mr. Douglass called them in. Snow or no snow, lessons were lessons and had to be learned.

Tom sat with his schoolbooks in front of him. There was no geography. People knew very little about a large part of the world. Tom's own father had just finished making one of the first maps of Virginia.

There was no history book on Tom's desk. Tom read history for fun. He didn't study it.

There was no arithmetic book on his desk. He had to make his own arithmetic book as he went along. He used big sheets of paper. Mrs. Douglass sewed them together for him. Mr. Douglass read him examples from his own book, which he had made the same way years ago. Tom copied them on a sheet of paper.

He had no lead pencil. He had to make his own pen, from a goose feather. He had to make his own ink, by mixing ink powder with vinegar. With his homemade ink and his homemade pen, he would work the example in his homemade book. Tom liked to make things though. And he liked arithmetic.

He had no geography. He had no arithmetic. He had no history. He had plenty of books on his desk without them. He had a Latin grammar, a Greek grammar, and a French grammar. He spent most of his time studying these.

Today it was hard to study. His eyes kept going toward the window. It had stopped snowing. The sun was out. Already water was dripping from the roof. Everything outside was a dazzling white. Tom looked at the snow. He wondered what his little mountain would look like in the snow. He made up his mind that someday he would find out.

"Tom Jefferson," said Mr. Douglass, "is your lesson ready?"

Tom jumped. He had forgotten all about his lessons. The other boys laughed. Tom bent over his books in a hurry.

Soon, though, he was peeping out of the window again. He could see the snow fort. It was only half-finished, and if school wasn't over very soon, would melt before they could use it at all. Tom remembered the time, back at Tuckahoe, when he had been a very little boy. He remembered how he had thought he could make dinnertime come by saying the Lord's Prayer, like a witch's spell. He almost laughed out loud when he remembered it.

He had found another way now to make time go by quickly. If he put his whole mind on what he was doing, he would forget about the time. He began to study his Latin again. This time he was very much in earnest. He put his

whole mind on it. He forgot about the snow.
He forgot about the time.

Almost before he knew what was happening,
Mr. Douglass was telling the boys they could
put their books up for the day.

They ran outdoors. They finished building
the fort. Then what a grand time the "Indians"

and the "Settlers" had! Which side won? That
didn't make any difference at all!

IN THE WOODS

That night Tom dreamed about the snowball
battle. He was leading the Indians. "Come on!
We'll storm the fort!"

Every snowball he threw made a *plop* when
it hit. That was strange. *Plop! Plop!*

He rolled over sleepily. The dream was gone,
but the *plop! plop!* was keeping on. At last
he opened his eyes. Then he sat up in bed to
listen. Something was going *plop! plop!* outside
the window. Suddenly he knew. The weather
had turned warm. The snow on the roof was
melting. It was dripping from the eaves. *Plop!*

He curled back under his blanket. There would
be no snow battles tomorrow. The fort would be
a slushy mess.

"So will the roads," he thought sleepily. "I hope Mrs. Douglass won't want to go anywhere tomorrow. Her carriage wheels would sink hub-deep in the mud. The horses would hardly be able to pull their own feet out. Yes, sir! To-morrow is going to be a fine day to stay in the house if this keeps up."

By the next afternoon he had changed his mind. It was true that the snow fort was now nothing but slush. The red clay mud was just as slippery and sticky as he had expected it to be. The sun was shining brightly and the wind was blowing. It was a very fine day to be outdoors.

"Come on, Tom," called John. "Let's go for a run in the woods. It will clear the cobwebs from your brain."

"Fine!" said Tom. "Just wait a minute. Let me see if this works. I'm trying to make a sewing box for Mrs. Douglass, with separate places for all the things she likes to keep in it. See!"

He held up four or five thin strips of wood. He had cut them with his knife so they would fit together. Now he was trying to make them all stand up at once. He twisted them and straightened them, but every time they fell down.

"There!" said John. "Now you've had all your work for nothing."

Tom shook his head. "No such thing! I've just learned another way how not to do it." He laughed. "I've learned four other ways how not to make it, already, but I can't expect to hit the right way the very first time I try. Tonight, when I start all over again, it is going to be a big help to know all the things I mustn't do."

John grinned. "You and your notions!" he teased Tom.

Tom didn't mind. "Oh, well," he said, "I always like to puzzle things out for myself."

The boys ran out in the yard. They started across the road. Once Tom thought he was stuck. It felt as if the mud were pulling his boots off his feet. Finally, though, they reached the other side.

The ground in the woods was wet and soft, It was easy to walk on. The pine needles were soft under foot.

Soon they came to the creek. Sometimes the creek was so small they could get across with a run and a jump. Sometimes they could get across on big steppingstones. Today, though, the creek was rushing along like a little river. It was too wide to jump over. The water had covered the steppingstones.

"Let's go upstream a little," said John. "Maybe we can find a place where it isn't so wide."

They went up the stream. It seemed to be just as wide, all the way.

Then Tom saw a big tree by the side of the creek. Its branches reached over the water. They were covered with wild grapevines.

"Look!" said Tom.

Some of the vines were as thick as a heavy rope. He reached out as far as he could over the water, and caught one of the vines. He tried it two or three times, to make sure it was strong enough to hold him. Then he pulled it back with both hands as far as he could.

Holding tight to the vine, he ran to the edge of the creek and jumped. The vine swung him across the creek. On the other side he let go and dropped. He landed safely on the bank. The vine swung back.

"Come on over," he called to John. "It's fun."

John came swinging across, too.

This time Tom caught the vine and fastened it in some bushes, so they could use it to get back.

"That was fun," said John. "I like to go whizzing through the air like that."

"So do I," said Tom. "I always like to do new things."

The boys walked on through the woods.

"Look!" said Tom. "Was that a bluebird over there in the bushes?"

"Maybe it was," said John.

"Let's go see."

The boys crept up close to the bushes. Something blue came whirring out. The bird flew up into the nearest tree.

"It *is* a bluebird!" cried Tom. "It is a week earlier than the first one I saw last year."

"How do you know?"

"I have a notebook, where I write down the first time I see each kind of bird. I write down when I hear the frogs croak for the first time. I write down when the first peach tree blooms."

"What good does all that do you?" asked John.

"Oh, I always like to keep track of things. Then I don't have to wonder about them. *I know.*"

Now they came to a little stream. They could see where it joined the big creek farther down.

The big creek was so deep it would be dangerous to play there, but the little stream was just
the right size for safety.

"Let's make a water wheel," said Tom. "I'll
show you how. You find two forked sticks and
one long, round one."

While John was hunting for the sticks, Tom
broke off a branch from a poplar tree, and
whittled six small flat pieces from the soft wood.
He cut one smooth round piece for the hub of the
wheel and made a hole through the center of it.
Then he cut six deep slits around the outside of
the hub, and into these slits he wedged the six flat
pieces. He ran the long round stick through the
hole in the middle. Now he had a paddle wheel
with six paddles.

"We'll push one of the forked sticks deep in
this soft, wet dirt on each side of the stream," he
told John. "Then we'll rest the ends of the long
stick in the forks. See!"

84

With each end of the stick resting in the forks, the wheel was right over the middle of the stream. The lowest paddle dipped into the water. It dipped in just a little too deep.

"We will have to raise the forked sticks just a little, John."

Now it wasn't deep enough.

"Let's push the forked sticks down a little farther."

There! That was just right.

The water, as it rushed along, pushed the lowest paddle forward. The wheel turned and the next paddle dropped down. The water pushed that one, too. Then the wheel began to turn faster and faster.

The boys stood up.

"Look," said Tom. "The sun is beginning to go down. It is time we started back."

"I hate to leave our water wheel, now that it is working so nicely," John told him.

85

"So do I, but the next time we come, we can make another one. I like to make things."

John laughed. "You certainly like to do a lot of things. You like to puzzle things out. You like to do things. You like to keep track of things. You like to make things."

"It's fun," said Tom.

A Hot Summer

IT WAS good to be back home for the summer. Home was a busy place. Tom's father was well-to-do. He owned a great deal of land. He had a good many servants. Nevertheless, even in the home of the well-to-do people, there was plenty of work for everybody.

There were no stores near Shadwell. There were no markets. There was no place where the Jeffersons could buy anything for miles and miles. Whatever they wanted they had to raise or make for themselves.

They made their own candles. They made their own soap. They made their own nails.

They raised their own sheep. There was one
sheep for each person. From the wool they spun
their own thread, to weave their own cloth, to
make their own clothes.

Every day Tom rode over the plantation with

his father. Land that had been covered with woods when he first went away to school had been cleared. The trees had been cut down. Then the land had been planted with tobacco and corn.

There were men and women working in the cornfields. There were men and women working in the tobacco fields. The men in charge told the workers what to do and how to do it, and Tom's father was in charge of them all. He checked every day to make sure that things were being done right.

By nine o'clock the sun was hot. By ten o'clock it was hotter still. The people in the fields worked under the blazing sun.

Tom had very fair skin. He didn't even tan the way many people do. His face would burn red. Then his skin would begin to peel. It was very uncomfortable. He was glad when Father turned back toward the big house.

It was warm, even there, but a stiff breeze came through the big open door in the hall. It ruffled his long red hair. Tom grinned. That felt good! Through the doorway he could look over the fields and woods to the little mountain.

"There is mighty apt to be a good breeze over there, right at the very top," he thought.

He sat down on the big hall sofa to cool off. It was only for a minute or two. Tom never liked to sit still very long without doing something. Besides, Father had asked him if he wouldn't help teach the little girls to write.

"I've been so busy that, really, they haven't had any schooling since we left Tuckahoe."

The girls were playing house down under the big pine tree. They had swept the fallen pine tags into ridges to make walls for their houses. They had gone down into the fields and brought back a basket of cockleburs. Cockleburs stuck

90

tightly to each other when they were pressed together. They could be made into chairs and tables and all sorts of doll furniture. The burs stuck to a little girl's fingers just as hard as they stuck to each other. How those prickers could hurt little fingers!

"I'm tired of making furniture," said Martha. "Let's play something else."

"What?"

Martha thought for a minute. Then she saw Tom coming down the path.

"Here comes Tom. He always has good ideas. Tom, what shall we play next?"

"How about playing school?"

He knew if he said, "Let me give you a writing lesson," they would have started fussing like angry blue jays. "Play school," though, was something different.

"How do we play?" they asked.

"I'll be the schoolmaster and I'll set each one

of you a lesson. You had better do it, too." Then he pretended to be very gruff and fierce. "If you don't——"

The girls laughed. The idea of Tom looking fierce was funny. They pretended to be afraid.

The oldest one dropped him a curtsy. "Yes, sir! I'll do my lesson. 'Deed, I will!"

The youngest little girl thought that it would be fun to play she was stubborn. "Tom, I don't see any sense in our having to learn to write."

"Books have to be written before they can be read. You wouldn't like to live in a world without books, would you?"

"I wouldn't care a bit."

"Suppose folks could never write letters to their friends."

"That wouldn't make any difference to me."

"It wouldn't? Well, if Father couldn't write, how would he ever be able to send an order to London for that spinet?"

92

They all laughed.

"Shall we play down here or up at the house?" asked Martha.

"I suppose we could play here. I could write your lesson for you with a stick on the ground. If we go up to the house I'll make each of you a book like the one Mrs. Douglass made me last winter for my arithmetic. You can write in your book every day. I'll make each of you a goose-quill pen for your very own."

Tom was forgetting that it was to be just a "play school." The little girls were forgetting it, too. They thought it would be quite exciting for each one of them to have a writing book all her very own.

They quickly threw down the stickery cockle-burs which they had been shaping into all sorts of doll furniture. They left the ridges of pine tags standing in place so that they could finish the walls of their playhouse some other time.

Then they followed Tom back to the house and upstairs to Mother's room.

The little girls sat down on low stools and waited for their make-believe "Schoolmaster" to start the game. Tom wrote a sentence at the top of a page for each of them.

"Now, you copy it all down the page. If it looks very clear and neat, we'll use it for the first page of your book."

The little girls were soon busy with their writing lesson. Tom got out his own book, so that he could be busy, too. After a while Big Sister Jane looked into the room to see what was keeping everybody so quiet.

"You mustn't interrupt, Jane," said Martha. "This is a schoolroom and we must be quiet. Tom, if Jane stays in here, you'll have to set her a lesson, too."

"All right," said Tom. "Look, Jane. Here is something one of the boys wrote out for me

94

last winter. Can you read it so that it makes good sense?"

He showed her a page from his notebook and pointed to a jingle written there.

I saw the sea all in a blaze of fire
I saw a house high as the moon and higher
I saw the sun at twelve o'clock at night
I saw the man who saw this wondrous sight.

Jane read it over. "No one could see the sea in a blaze, or a house high as the moon—or the sun at twelve o'clock at night, either. It is just plain nonsense!"

"No, it isn't, Jane. It is all true. Try reading it once again."

She read it again. She read it a third time. Then she began to laugh. "I see. You just have to watch where you end each sentence. Then it makes good sense."

"Right," said Tom. "Now read it."

"I saw the sea.
    All in a blaze of fire I saw a house.
    High as the moon and higher I saw the sun.
    At twelve o'clock at night I saw the man
        who saw this wondrous sight."

"It certainly does make a difference where you put your periods, doesn't it, Tom? I'll remember that the next time I write you a letter."

Just then the houseboy came to tell them that dinner was ready. The little girls dropped their quill pens in a hurry. Tom's writing school was over for the day.

A HOT AFTERNOON

The dining room was hot. It was on the sunny side of the house. Very little breeze came in through the open windows. Plenty of flies did. Tom was used to flies. He took them as a matter of course, as everyone else did.

There was ham for dinner. There was fried chicken. There were corn, beans, and radishes from the garden.

Just as they sat down at the table Father's friend, Mr. Harris, came riding down the lane. That meant, of course, that dinner must wait while Father went to greet him. It must wait until Mr. Harris could go to the guest chamber and wash up. At last he was ready to sit down, too.

Mr. Harris usually came over from his plantation in Louisa County to see Father every week. For the last two months, though, he had been on a trip to Alexandria. This was his first visit since he had come back.

He would spend the night, to give his horse a chance to rest. He would go home tomorrow after dinner. Then, in a few days, Father would go to see him. They visited each other like that nearly every week.

Children weren't supposed to talk at the

table, but Tom didn't care. He would much rather listen, anyway.

Today the talk was so exciting he almost forgot to eat the hot buttered corn. Mr. Harris had watched Braddock's army when it marched out from Alexandria.

Tom had heard all about Braddock's army and why it came to Virginia. He knew that the King of England said that all the land on the other side of the mountains belonged to England. The King of France said that it belonged to France. He sent his soldiers to build forts and to drive the English settlers back.

Sometimes the Indians helped the English, but most of the time they helped the French. They had begun to kill the men who had built homes beyond the mountains. They were killing the women and children. Something had to be done to stop them.

The King of England had sent General Brad-

dock over with a thousand soldiers. They were going to drive the French away from their forts. Mr. Harris had seen them start.

"They were a fine sight, in all their red uniforms," he said, "but I didn't like the way General Braddock talked. He seemed to think the British soldiers were so much better than the Virginians. He said that *we* may have had trouble with the Indians, but they'll be afraid as soon as they see *his* men. He wouldn't even listen when we told him that Indians don't fight the way white men do."

"I understand young Washington has gone with him," said Father. "He is the young man who carried Governor Dinwiddie's message all the way across the mountains to the French commander on the Ohio River two years ago. *He* knows Indians and understands the way they fight. Maybe he can make General Braddock listen to common sense."

"I certainly hope so," said Mr. Harris.

"If the army started last May," said Father, "we ought to hear some news about them almost any day, now."

After dinner the house grew very quiet. The girls all went to their rooms for a nap. They covered their beds wth mosquito netting, to keep the flies and mosquitoes from bothering them. Soon, all was quiet.

Father and Mr. Harris sat in the big, wide hall. Sometimes they talked. Sometimes even they nodded a bit, too.

Tom got a book from Father's bookshelf. When he was a little boy, he had thought books were just things you had to study. He knew better than that now. He knew what fun it was to read. Father let him take any of the books he wanted. When he had finished reading them, he would start all over again.

Caesar hated to see young Mister Tom get

started with a book. Caesar thought it was a waste of time to read, when there were so many other things to do. They could go swimming in the creek. Mister Tom was a good swimmer. It was a shame for him to sit there with his nose stuck in a book all through the afternoon.

Caesar knew that there wasn't a bit of use in trying to get him away, though. When Mister Tom started reading, he kept on reading.

Caesar went out into the yard and lay down under a big locust tree. The bees buzzed in the warm sun. Pretty soon Caesar was asleep.

It was cooler in the late afternoon. The little girls, fresh from their naps, played house again underneath the pine trees.

Tom got out his paper and drawing board, and began to work on some plans he had started.

All the homes that Tom had ever seen, except Tuckahoe, were small places. Many of them were made of logs. They had four walls, a chimney, a door, and two or three windows. That was all. They weren't the least bit pretty. In one of Father's books Tom had found pictures of beautiful houses in other countries. He was trying to draw plans of houses like those. Someday, maybe, he would be able to build himself a house like them, too.

The older girls sat in the big hall and sewed. Jane was making ruffles for the cuffs of Father's shirt. Mary was hemming some bands for Tom's shirts. They sewed until it was too dark to see. Tom had to put up his drawing board.

Then they all watched the big moon come up, until it was high over the locust trees, casting its mellow light over the land.

"Caesar," called Father, "bring Mister Tom his fiddle."

Caesar smiled. "Yes, sir!" he said.

Caesar liked to hear Mister Tom play the fiddle. He could play hymn tunes, but he could play jig tunes, too, and he knew that nothing pleased Caesar more than hearing them.

Caesar brought the fiddle. Tom tucked it under his chin. He began to play. The girls sang. Caesar sat out on the porch steps. It seemed to him that anybody should know this was more fun than reading all the time!

A Storm and
a Defeat

THE NEXT afternoon Tom decided he would go for a swim. The day was hot. The sun was glaring. In the woods green branches would hide the sun. The water would be cool.

It was over two years now since he and Caesar had found the pool and the little cavelike place beyond it. How they had worked that summer!

They had pulled and shoved the rocks from the middle of the pool until they had pushed them down into the brook. Then they plastered them with mud until they made a dam. The dam backed the water into the pool. It still wasn't up over a boy's head, but it was deep enough to do some good loud splashing in. It was deep enough to swim in, too.

They had dug footholds in the hard dirt between the rocks on the steep hillside, so they could climb like goats up to the cavelike place between the two biggest rocks. Tom had put up some shelves so he would have a place for the rocks he was collecting around the farm. There were some arrowheads, too, that he had found in the fields.

There was a clear trail down from the house to the swimming pool now. The boys' feet had made it. They often went down together. Sometimes, though, Tom liked to go alone. It gave him time to think.

"What about?" Jane had teased him once.

"Oh, everything! Birds and Indians and wild animals and how many kinds of weeds there are on the farm and how fast the corn is growing and the best places to find wild turkeys and why

105

do hens lay more eggs than eagles do and whether Liza Ann is cooking Sally Lunn for supper—you know, all sorts of things like that."

"It is a wonder you even get home if you have all that to think about."

"Oh, I reckon sometimes I just fall asleep."

Today, Tom splashed around, then lay down and let the cool water ripple over his feet.

Soon he jumped up. He grabbed his clothes from the bushes by the pool and began to climb up to the cavelike place. His shirt and trousers were homespun, and it took precious little time for him to dress.

Then he sat down on the biggest rock. A hawk flew lazily high in the sky. Something rustled in the bushes—a partridge, maybe. He watched for only a moment, but he wasn't really interested in birds now.

His mind was still full of Mr. Harris' stories about General Braddock.

"Suppose," thought Tom, "that General Braddock *doesn't* drive the French back. Suppose the Indians come over the mountains. Will they reach Shadwell? Of course General Braddock won't be defeated—not with all those fine soldiers. I wish I could have seen them. I wish—"

He was startled by a loud clap of thunder. His back had been turned toward the direction in

107

which the storm was gathering. Now he saw dark clouds driving across the sky.

At first he thought he would stay right there until the storm was over. The he remembered that the little girls were afraid of thunder. He decided to try to make it to the house before the rain started.

He climbed down in a jiffy. He ran through the woods and across the field. Just as he reached the house it began to pour.

Tom sank down to the doorstep to catch his breath. Then he jumped up. Someone was galloping down the lane. It was Mr. Harris. He must have started home, and then decided to come back to wait until the storm was over.

BRADDOCK'S DEFEAT

Father came hurrying to the door. "Come in," he called, "before you are soaked to the skin."

108

Something more important than the rain had brought Mr. Harris back.

"Braddock's army," he cried, "was surprised by the Indians! Braddock and nearly all his men were killed! The news has just reached the courthouse. I hurried back to tell you."

"What happened?" asked Tom.

"There was a fight. General Braddock insisted on fighting the English way. He kept his men out in an open field. The Indians were hidden behind trees. They could shoot without being seen by the English.

"Mr. Washington had two horses shot from under him. He had four bullets go through his coat, but he wasn't even hurt. He and his men knew how to fight the Indian way. They hid behind trees, too. They slipped from one tree to another. They kept the Indians back until what was left of Braddock's army could get together again."

"What will happen now?" asked Martha. "Will the Indians kill all the poor women and children in the Valley? Will they come over the mountains and kill us, too?"

"Mr. Washington can stop them," said Tom.

"I believe he can," his father told him. "And the time has come when the people in this country must learn to take care of themselves."

Martha was too young to understand that. The only thing that worried her was whether the Indians would keep on killing people. Since Tom said Mr. Washington wouldn't let them, she didn't care about the rest.

Tom cared, though, and he remembered his father's words—"The time has come when the people in this country must learn to take care of themselves."

A Chance for Eb

Toм stood at the window and looked out through the small glass panes. It was a beautiful day outside, but Tom was very sad. Father was dead.

Beyond the fields the sun shone brightly on the little mountain. It was Tom's very own little mountain now. So was Shadwell, with its fields and its woods and its buildings. Father had left them all to him. But oh, how Tom missed Father!

Baby Randolph and his twin sister Nancy were playing on the floor. Jane was watching them.

Father had left Baby Randolph his farm on the James River, but Randolph was too little to know anything about farms. He wasn't two years old yet. He was too little even to know that Father was gone. He and Nancy rolled and tumbled on the floor and were as happy as two little puppies.

Tom stood looking at his little mountain. Fall had come. Most of the leaves were red or yellow. The pines stayed deep, dark green. It was beautiful, but not even his little mountain could keep Tom from feeling sad.

"Let me bring you your fiddle, Mister Tom," said Caesar. "Play something for us."

Tom shook his head.

"Do, Tom," said Jane. "We'll play and sing the hymns that Father liked."

"All right," said Tom.

Caesar brought him his fiddle. Tom played the hymns that Father liked. Jane sang them. It made them both feel better.

"Tom, you know that Father wanted you to go back to school," said Jane.

"I know," Tom told her, "but I am fourteen years old now. There are six girls in the family, and Randolph and I are the only boys. Randolph is just a baby. Don't you think I ought to stay and take care of you all?"

"Not yet," said Jane. "You ought to finish school first."

Tom was glad Jane said that. He wanted to go back to school, himself. Father had wanted him to go. If only he could be nearer home!

"There is a place nearer than Mr. Douglass'," Jane said. "Mr. Maury is taking some boys to teach. He is only fourteen miles away."

That would be fine! Of course, Tom couldn't go back and forth every day. He could come back for a day or two, every now and then, when the roads were good. He would be close by, if they needed him.

He was sure that was what Father would have wanted him to do.

In a very short while, Tom left for Peter's Mountain. He was going to school at Mr. Maury's.

LET'S GO FISHING

The boys at Mr. Maury's school studied hard while they studied, but when their lessons were over they played hard, too.

They rode and climbed over Peter's Mountain. They went hunting in the woods. They went fishing in the mountain streams. They brought back wild turkey and squirrel and fish for Mrs. Maury's table. Sometimes they would even bring back a deer.

One day, while the boys were studying, a letter came for Mr. Maury. After he had read it, he rapped on his desk for attention.

The boys looked up from their books.

"I must go to the courthouse tomorrow, on

114

business," said Mr. Maury. "If you do your work well today, you may have a holiday then."

Tom studied harder than ever. He knew just how he wanted to spend his holiday. Tomorrow he would go fishing.

He talked with his friend Lewis about it at dinnertime. "Let's leave right after breakfast. We'll build a fire and cook some of the fish we catch for lunch, so we won't need to take anything with us but some bread."

They left the next morning right after breakfast. They went deep into the woods until they came to a clear stream. They cut themselves two fishing poles and dug worms for bait.

All the morning long they fished up and down the stream. First they tried one place. Then they tried another. They had a fine time, but they didn't catch any fish.

When dinnertime came, Lewis said, "Let's eat our bread, even if we haven't any fish."

115

Tom shook his head. "I want fish. Let's go up the stream and try once more."

They went on up the stream, until they came to a big rock.

Tom stopped short. "I smell fish," he said. "I smell fish *cooking*."

"Look!" said Lewis.

Back of the big rock rose a thin line of smoke.

The boys climbed over the rock. On the other side they saw a boy about their own age. He had been fishing, too. His luck had been better than theirs. He was going to have fish for dinner.

"Hello!" called Tom.

The boy looked up. "Hello," he said.

Tom scrambled down the rock. "Why, I know you. You're the boy who brought back Mrs. Maury's cow when it was lost in the woods last month. She said your name was Eb."

Eb grinned, but said nothing. They could see he was shy, but he was friendly, too.

"Come on, Tom," called Lewis. "We'd better be getting along up the stream."

"Look here," Tom said to Eb, "you have plenty of fish, but no bread. We have plenty of bread, but no fish. Let's have dinner together."

Eb was quite willing for them to have dinner together. Soon enough fish for three hungry boys was broiling over the fire.

At first Tom had to do most of the talking. Eb said very little.

Eb knew that Tom and Lewis were two of the young gentlemen from Mr. Maury's school. He knew that only rich men's sons could afford to go to school. He knew that, while they were wearing rough clothes now, no better than his own, at home they had suits of velvet and satin. Eb wanted to be friends, but he felt awkward.

Soon, though, Tom had Eb talking, too. Almost everyone liked to talk to Tom because he was so interested in what they had to say.

Eb told how he and his granddad lived in a cabin back up on the mountainside.

"Granddad used to be a hunter," he said. "He has been away beyond the Blue Mountains."

Tom nodded. "My father crossed the Blue Mountains, too, once."

"Granddad certainly can tell some wonderful stories about what he saw on the other side. He's so old and he's told them so often he doesn't know himself how much is true and how much he has just imagined."

Tom laughed. He had heard that very old people tell stories like that.

"You ought to hear him tell about a bridge he saw there. 'The Giant's Bridge,' he calls it."

"I'd like to hear about it."

"Granddad is so crippled with rheumatism now he can hardly move around the cabin. He gets powerful lonesome with just him and me by ourselves all the time. He certainly would like

to have somebody new to listen to him tell about that bridge."

"How did you say you get to your cabin?" asked Tom. "I'm coming the first chance I get."

Eb was delighted. "Granddad will be glad to see you."

After dinner was over, before he started back up the mountain, Eb showed them the best pools to fish in. Soon Tom and Lewis had bites on their lines, too.

"You're not really going to see Eb and his old grandfather, are you?" asked Lewis, while they were fishing.

"Of course I am. Why not?"

"I shouldn't think you'd bother with people like that. Why, I don't believe Eb can even read or write. His great-grandfather probably had to sell himself as a servant for six years to pay the captain who brought him over here from England. And *your* great-grandfather was William

Randolph of Turkey Island! He was one of the richest and best-known men in all Virginia."

"Shucks!" said Tom. "What do I care about great-grandfathers? It is Eb I am going to see. Maybe he hasn't had a chance to go to school, but he's a better fisherman than either of us. He shared his dinner with us, didn't he? He's a fine fellow and I like him. He's my friend."

AT THE CABIN BACK IN THE WOODS

The first afternoon that Tom could get away he started out to find Eb's cabin. It was a very small cabin and far back in the woods, but at last he found it.

Eb and his grandfather had just finished dinner. Their round wooden dishes were still on the table, and Eb was wiping off two big knives.

"What's become of your forks?" asked Tom.

"Forks!" said the old man. "Who wants

forks? We never had such new-fangled notions when I was a boy."

"Oh!" said Tom.

"They're nonsense," the old man grumbled. "When I'm so old I can't use my knife, feed me spoon-meat, but don't bring me a fork."

"I won't," Eb promised him.

"Another thing I don't like," said the old man, "is all this talk about china dishes. Who wants china dishes? They make your knife dull, scraping against them. No, sir, give me a good wooden dish every time."

"What about pewter dishes?" asked Tom.

"They're all right, too. They don't break, and, if they get any dents in them, you can melt them down and turn them into something else. But I don't want any of these china dishes!"

"All right," said Eb, "we won't have china dishes. They'd be broken, anyhow, before we could get them all the way from Williamsburg."

The old man seemed to want to find fault with everything. Tom was afraid he hadn't chosen a very good day to make his visit.

" 'All the way from Williamsburg!' " the old man grumbled. "Why, that's no distance at all. Wait until you've crossed the mountains the way I have. Then you can talk about distance."

"That's why I came to see you," said Tom. "I thought maybe you'd tell me about some of the things you've seen across the mountains."

The old man was pleased, but he wasn't going to show it. He kept on grumbling.

"H-m-m," he said. "It isn't such a big thing to go across the mountains any more. Lots of people are moving over there now. They're coming down the Valley as thick as grasshoppers. When I was a young man, it was different. Back in 1716—when Governor Spottswood and his friends saw the Valley for the first time—it was more important then."

"You are the only man *I* know who has ever seen it," said Tom. "I mean, besides Father."

That seemed to please the old man.

"I've seen it, all right," he said, "and more than once, too. I've seen some strange things over there in the Valley."

"What is the most wonderful thing you have ever seen there?"

The old man thought it over for a minute or two. "Well," he said, "I reckon the most wonderful thing I ever saw was The Bridge."

"What is so wonderful about a bridge?"

"I didn't say *a* bridge. I said *The* Bridge.

"The Lord made it. It is a natural bridge. There is a creek running under it. Some folks say the creek must have cut its way through the rock. I don't know. But The Bridge is made of solid rock, and it is so high you could put a church underneath it, steeple and all."

Tom closed his eyes. He tried to imagine a

bridge made of solid rock, so high you could put a church under it, steeple and all.

"When I was there eight or ten years ago," the old man said, "there was a young fellow named George Washington——"

"George Washington!" cried Tom. "Why, he's the one who kept the Indians back when General Braddock was defeated!"

The old man didn't like to be interrupted. "Maybe he is," he grunted, "but he wasn't any soldier then. He was a surveyor."

"What does a surveyor do?" asked Eb.

"He draws the line between your land and your neighbors'," Tom told him. "My father was a surveyor."

"Look here," said the old man, "are you telling this story or am I?"

"I'm sorry," said Tom, "I didn't mean to interrupt. Please go on."

"Well, it doesn't make any difference whether

he was a soldier or a surveyor or anything else. I met a hunter who told me this young Washington stood down by the creek and threw a rock over the bridge. I don't believe it. It's too high. When you stand on top and look over the edge, it makes you dizzy.

"I certainly would like to see that bridge again. It is just about the grandest thing I ever did see."

Eb walked part of the way back with Tom, to show him a short cut.

"Do you suppose," asked Eb, "there really is a bridge like that, or is Granddad making it up?"

"It's there, all right," said Tom. "I've heard Father talk about it. When I grow up, I'm going to see it, myself."

"I wish I could," said Eb. He kicked at a pebble in his path. "I'd like to be a surveyor like that Mr. Washington."

"Well," said Tom, "why can't you? If you study hard enough——"

"I don't know how to study. I can't even read or write. Neither can Granddad. And you have to have someone to show you how."

"Haven't you ever been to school?"

Eb shook his head. "There aren't any schools for poor folks like us. Schools are just for rich men's sons."

"That's not fair."

"Maybe it's not, but I reckon it will stay that way until someone cares enough to do something about it."

They had reached the big stone.

"You know the way from here," Eb said. "I'd better be going back. Good-by."

"Good-by."

Eb started back up the hill. He was a big boy. Probably he would never learn how to read and write, now.

Tom started down the stream. He was going back to his books. It wasn't fair, he thought, for him to be able to go to school, just because his father had money.

"It ought to be so that Eb could go to school, too," thought Tom. "And all the other boys like Eb ought to be able to go."

All the way back to Mr. Maury's Tom thought and thought about it.

PLANS FOR THE FUTURE

Mr. Maury was away again. There were no lessons to be studied that evening. The boys all sat around the big open fire.

"Get your fiddle," Lewis called to Tom, "and give us a tune."

Tom brought out his fiddle and played lively tunes that set their feet tapping. Still he was thinking about Eb.

When he stopped, the boys began to talk about what they would do when they grew up.

128

"I shall be a minister," said Sam. "I shall go to England to study. Then the king will send me back to one of the churches in Virginia."

"I shall be a planter," said Hugh. "I shall have a big plantation, and grow tobacco and corn and wheat."

"I shall be a soldier," said Will. "I'll drive the Indians back over the mountains."

"What are you going to do?" they asked Tom.

"Tom won't have to do anything," Lewis told them. "His father left him plenty of money, land, and servants. He can stay home and do nothing."

Everyone laughed. They all knew that Tom Jefferson was up to something every minute of the day. It was a joke even to think of his staying at home and doing nothing.

"Tom will work all right," said Sam. "He'll work hard to get more money to buy more fields to raise more tobacco to get more money to buy more fields——"

"Not Tom!" declared Will. "He won't grow anything as ordinary as tobacco. He'll spend all his time trying out new ideas and inventions, the way he does now."

Tom grinned. He didn't mind being teased. "Maybe I shall," he told them. "And maybe *some* of my new ideas will work."

"You'll make yourself plans for a new home, too. None of the ordinary houses around here will suit you, and you're always drawing plans for something or other, you know."

"He'll build his home on top of that little mountain he is always talking about," Sam suggested knowingly.

They all laughed again.

"Say, that's a good idea," said Tom. "The mosquitoes will never bite me up that high."

"You'd never be able to get away in bad weather. The snow and the mud would keep you shut in for weeks."

130

"I wouldn't mind staying on my little mountain all the time."

"Yes, you would—because you want to go on long journeys. You want to cross the Blue Mountains, you know, and see The Giant's Bridge you were telling us about at supper."

The bridge reminded Tom of Eb again. He stopped laughing. The other boys grew serious.

"Let's stop joking," said Sam. "What do you really want to do when you grow up, Tom?"

Tom knew what he wanted to do, but it was a little hard to explain.

"I want to fix things so that boys like Eb will have the same chance we do."

"Isn't it exactly like you to think up some wild notion like that? How would you go about it, I'd like to know?"

"Well, the first thing would be schools. A boy ought to be able to go to school, no matter whether his father is rich or poor."

"I believe maybe you're right about that. What next?"

"I'm not sure. You can't think a thing like that out in a hurry."

"You certainly can't," agreed Sam, "but if you're going to see to it that everybody has an equal chance, you've cut out some work for yourself that is harder by a jugful than anything we were planning for you to do."

"Maybe it is—but it is more important, too."

Too Much Company

THE SKY in the east was just beginning to grow light. The birds in the locust tree outside Tom's window were beginning to stir and to twitter. Down in the barnyard, the chickens were waking. A rooster crowed.

Tom rolled over and opened his eyes. He could see the clock across the room. Goodness! If it was light enough to see the clock it was time to get up! He sat up quickly.

Tom was back home again, but he was still studying hard. There was a lot of work he wanted to do today.

The early morning air was chilly. Tom hurried to the fireplace and lighted the fire. He always liked to make his own fire.

When the fire was crackling and blazing, he looked at the clock again. Caesar didn't like getting up early nearly so well as Tom did. It would probably be quite a while before he brought Tom his water to wash with. That would give Tom some time to study. He sat down at his desk with his books.

It seemed to him almost no time before Caesar came. Then, while he finished dressing, he could hear breakfast being brought into the dining room from the kitchen out in the yard. He could smell the hot corn bread and bacon. It made him forget all about studying—for a little while, at least.

After breakfast, though, he went back to his room. "I'm going to put in a good, hard day at my books," he told Jane.

"That's fine," said Jane.

Tom sat down to study. He was just getting nicely started when Caesar knocked at the door.

"Mister Tom!" said Caesar, "there's company coming down the lane."

Tom was head of the house now. It would never do to let company come without welcoming them himself. He went down to the big hall. There were Uncle Isham and Cousin John.

"We were on our way to the courthouse," said Uncle Isham. "We just stopped to rest our horses and see how you are getting along. We will stay only a few minutes."

They sat down and began to talk. Tom enjoyed talking with them. Before anybody realized, they had been there for two hours.

As soon as they had gone, Tom hurried back to his books. He was just opening his geometry, when Caesar came to the door.

Caesar looked happy. "Mister Tom," he said, "I tell you more company is coming down the lane now."

Tom put his pen down again. He went back downstairs. A big coach was stopping in front of the house. It was drawn by four horses.

"It is the Ballard coach," said Jane. "It must be Mrs. Ballard and her three daughters. You know—they are the ones who live over near Piney Mountain."

Tom hurried to open the door of the coach. He helped Mrs. Ballard and her daughters out.

"We are going to visit my sister," said Mrs. Ballard, "but we couldn't drive by without stopping for a little while."

"Of course not," said Mother. "You must stay to dinner."

Mrs. Ballard and her daughters had expected to stay to dinner. When people went traveling in Virginia in those days they always stopped at the nearest house when dinnertime came. Even if they weren't expected, they knew their hostess would be glad to see them.

Mrs. Ballard's coachman unharnessed the horses and led them around to the stable. Then he went to the kitchen for his dinner.

Jane took Mrs. Ballard and the girls upstairs to take off their bonnets. They came down just as dinner was being put on the table.

Four extra people for dinner didn't bother

Mrs. Jefferson at all. She was used to it. The table was always big enough for three or four extra plates.

After dinner, they all sat around in the big hall and talked. It was nearly four o'clock before the coachman brought the horses around again. The ladies said good-by and went on their way.

Almost before the coach was gone, Tom was back upstairs. "Here the day is nearly gone," he told Caesar, "and I haven't got a thing done. I *must* get to my study now!"

"Yes, Mister Tom. You certainly must."

Caesar tiptoed out of the room, since he had to be quiet whenever Tom was studying.

In a few minutes he was back. "Mister Tom, more company's coming!"

Tom put down his pen. He went to the window. Down the lane came Will and Sam, his old friends at Mr. Maury's.

They looked up and saw him. "Hello, there!" they called. "Come on down. We've just time for a brisk ride before sunset!"

Tom sent for his horse to be saddled. They had a fine ride before sunset. The boys came back to spend the night with him. He enjoyed every minute of it—but it wasn't studying!

Tom talked with Jane about it the next day, after the boys were gone.

"I wouldn't mind missing a day from my books every now and then," he told her, "but it is like this nearly every day. How do you ever get anything done, Jane?"

"Well," said Jane, "of course it is only when you are home that it is like this. Most of these folks are coming to see you."

"Oh," said Tom. He hadn't thought about it that way before.

If all this company was really his, it wasn't fair to his brothers and sisters. Company was really expensive. He had to feed their horses out in the stables. He had to feed their servants in the kitchen. It cost a lot of money. It wasn't fair to the family for them to have to take care of his company like that.

Tom thought things over for quite a while. He talked with his cousin about it. He wrote to one of Father's friends. At last he made up his mind.

There was only one college in all Virginia at that time. It was much farther away from home than Tom had ever been before. He would not have so much company there. He would be able to study better. He would make new friends.

Tom made up his mind to go to the College of William and Mary.

Caesar Was Wrong

"MISTER TOM," said Caesar, "are you sure your coattails are long enough?"

"Of course," said Tom. He was busy deciding what books to take to college with him. Caesar was packing his clothes.

"You sure your shoe buckles are big enough? Mister Tom?"

Tom laughed. "Are my shoe buckles so very important, Caesar?"

Caesar nodded his head. "Yes, sir! We want all your clothes to look like they just came over from London. We want them to be the very latest style."

"Caesar, you know that folks won't expect a boy from the backwoods to be dressed in the latest style," Tom told him.

"No, sir, they won't expect it, but we have to show them."

Caesar folded Tom's suit of light blue silk. The trousers came just to the knee. There were silver buttonholes and silver garters. There was a soft silk shirt with lace ruffles to wear with it. Caesar liked to see Mister Tom all dressed up in the handsome suit.

Of course, when Tom rode away from Shadwell, he wore a dark suit. He wore a heavy cape over his shoulders. His hat had a broad brim. In good weather, he would catch the brim up, by three loops of cord, to a button on the top. Then it was a three-cornered, cocked hat. When it rained, he could let the brim down. Then the rain couldn't beat in his face or run down the back of his neck.

It was December when Tom started for college. From Shadwell to Williamsburg was a long trip by horseback, over a hundred miles. No wonder Christmas caught him on the way.

Tom didn't mind. He was going to stop at Colonel Dandridge's home in Hanover County.

Christmas time was fun, when you were a boy, but when you were a young man, it was more fun still. Tom was old enough to go to dances now. He was old enough to sit with the men, after dinner, and join in the grown-up talk, instead of being sent off with the children. He was sure he was going to enjoy his visit.

After he reached Colonel Dandridge's, he wasn't quite so sure. There were ever so many people there. Some of them were his cousins, but he had never seen them before. They all knew one another and he didn't know anybody. It made him feel awkward and shy.

144

The house was so full of company that the schoolhouse in the yard had been turned into a guest room for the young men. Tom went out there with the others, to get ready for dinner. They were all talking about things he had never heard of. They had jokes he didn't understand.

Tom began to feel uncomfortable and left out. He began to worry about his clothes. Maybe Caesar had been right. Maybe they weren't like the things the other boys were wearing. He wondered if he ought to have pointed instead of square-toed shoes. He wondered if he had enough lace on his ruffles. Did the other boys think he looked odd?

There was so much company, there wasn't room enough for them all in the dining room at the same time. The ladies sat down first. Then, while the ladies were dressing for the dance, the gentlemen had their dinner.

Still more company began to come for the

dance. Tom looked around the table at the other men. Some of them wore wigs. Some of them had their own hair powdered white and tied in the back with a black ribbon. Their coats were of velvet and silk, in rich red and purple and blue. How fine they all looked!

There was one man, however, who didn't look fine at all. He was awkward and homely. He pronounced his words in a way that made even Tom smile. He called "earth" "yearth," and "learning" "larning." He looked every bit as countrified as Tom felt.

The stranger, though, didn't worry about his looks. Neither did anyone else. When he talked, everybody listened. When he laughed, everyone laughed with him.

"Who is he?" Tom asked his neighbor at the table curiously.

"His name is Patrick Henry. He has been a storekeeper here in the neighborhood, but his store has just failed."

"Oh," thought Tom, "then it isn't because he is rich that people like him. I wonder why it is."

His neighbor kept on talking, almost as if he had heard the question Tom was thinking.

"I suspect Patrick Henry is just about the most popular man in this room. He can make you laugh with him. He can make you cry with him. And you should hear him when he gets to talking about liberty! Yes, sir, he is a fine fellow!"

"He doesn't look so fine." Tom hadn't meant to say it out loud. He was startled when his neighbor answered him.

"Look here, young man. You are going to make a lot of mistakes in life if you go around judging birds by their feathers."

"I know it," said Tom.

"It is the man inside the clothes that counts and don't you forget it!"

The fiddles in the ballroom began to tune up.

It was time for the dance to begin. The girls were coming down the stairs.

Tom went into the ballroom with the others. He wasn't worried any longer about his clothes. What difference did it make if some of the other men had more lace on their ruffles than he did? He didn't even bother to notice their shoes. "I'd much rather be a lark than a peacock any day," he decided.

Then he forgot to think about himself. He danced the dignified minuet. He danced the lively country dances. He had a wonderful time.

College Student

DURING THE rest of Tom's visit at Colonel Dandridge's home, he and Mr. Henry saw a good deal of each other. They played their fiddles together for the others to dance. They went hunting in the pine woods. They joked and talked about everything under the sun.

They didn't think alike about a good many things, but on one thing they always agreed. They both loved liberty. They both thought that all men were born free and equal. They both thought that all men should be allowed to govern themselves, instead of being forced to obey laws they had no share in making.

There was so much for them to talk about that they were nowhere near through when Tom had to start on for Williamsburg. Mr. Henry said he would visit him the first time he had a chance.

After he left Colonel Dandridge's home, Tom's road led him through Richmond. Richmond was a very new and a very small city then, but it was the first city Tom had ever seen. He had never seen as many as twenty homes close together before. Indeed, little Richmond looked very big to him.

Williamsburg was bigger. Tom was bewildered. There were nearly two hundred houses! Its main street was three-quarters of a mile long! Almost a thousand people lived there.

It was a busy time of the year. The House of Burgesses was about to meet. From all over the colony the men who had been elected to the House were coming into town. Many of them brought their wives and daughters with them.

150

There would be plenty of balls and parties in Williamsburg during the next few weeks.

Tom was sure he had never seen so many fine clothes in all the days of his life put together. Silks and satins, laces and buckles! Well, he could get some fine clothes himself, but he didn't intend wearing them all the time. He liked his plain homespun clothes, too.

The Capitol was a big building. So were some of the homes. However, not even Tom could call the college big. The room they gave him was small, with bare plastered walls. It wasn't nearly so comfortable as his room back at Shadwell.

He didn't care about that, though. He liked a bare room when he was studying. He didn't want anything around that would take his attention from his books.

He had expected to be homesick and maybe he was at first, just a little. Dabney Carr was at the college, though. He and Tom had gone to

Mr. Maury's school together. When Tom wanted to talk about home he talked to Dabney.

Soon he made new friends. There was John Page, for instance. John's family lived across the river. He kept a small boat so that he could sail across to see them every now and then. Tom went with him sometimes.

Not all of his new friends were young people. Older men, too, found it interesting to talk to him. Williamsburg was the capital of Virginia. The governor lived there. His Palace was the finest home in the city. One of the governor's best friends was a professor at the college. He told the governor about his young student from the up-country. "He talks well. He knows how to listen. He is very fond of music."

Soon the governor, himself, began to invite Tom to the Palace. Sometimes he would ask Tom to bring his fiddle and play with some of the other guests who liked music.

There were other parties and balls, too. Tom tried to go to all of them. Before he had been in college a year he was having a very good time.

I'M SPENDING TOO MUCH

Good times cost money.

Dabney Carr knocked at Tom's door late one morning.

"Come in," called Tom.

Dabney opened the door. Tom was sitting at his desk. He was busy with his pen and paper.

"You've been sitting there all the morning, studying," said Dabney. "Let's go for a sail on the river with John."

"I am not studying exactly," said Tom. "I am just adding up some figures."

"So that is what makes you look so serious! Won't they add up right?"

"They add up right enough, I am afraid. That

153

is the trouble. I had no idea I had spent so much money, Dabney, since I have been in college."

"You are very fond of a good horse," Dabney reminded him.

"I know it. I didn't come here just to ride a good horse. I have plenty of those back home."

"And you didn't really need that brown velvet suit you had made last month."

"I don't suppose I did," Tom agreed, "or my new silver buckles, either. They didn't seem to cost so much by themselves, but when you add them all together—whew!"

"You will have to turn over a new leaf," Dabney told him. "If you just make up your mind that you won't spend so much after this———"

"I'll have to do better than that. You see, one of the reasons I came here was because I was spending more than my share of the money at home. It wasn't fair to the others. Now I've been spending more than my share here."

154

"What can you do about it, now?"

Tom picked up his pen. "I'm going to write Colonel Walker," he said. "Colonel Walker is taking care of things at home until I am twenty-one. I am going to ask him not to pay for what I have bought from the money that belongs to the family. He can take it out of the money that will come to me when I am twenty-one. That is the only fair way to do it."

Tom began to write. Dabney picked up a book to read while he waited for him. The room was quiet except for the scratching of the pen.

"There!" said Tom.

He put down his pen, then poured sand over the wet ink, to dry it. He folded the page and fastened it together with sealing wax and pressed his ring on the soft wax to make it hold. He wrote the address on the back of the letter. Paper was too scarce to use for a separate envelope.

"There!" said Tom. "That is done. Now I

feel better. Come on! Let's go for that sail on the river."

A LONG DAY'S WORK

When Tom studied, he didn't just read his book to see how soon he could get through with it. He read very carefully, stopping to think back every now and then. He kept his pen and his notebook close by. He wrote down the main ideas as he came to them. When he finished his book, he knew everything that was in it.

When he wrote, he wrote very carefully. He chose the exact words he needed. He made every sentence clear, so that it said exactly what he meant. He became so interested when he studied this way he forgot all about the time.

One evening he worked until it was too dark to see. He hated to stop even long enough to light a candle. When he walked over to the fireplace to get a light, he found he was stiff from sitting still so long. His eyes were tired, too.

He remembered how his father used to say, "You must have a trained mind in a strong body." He realized that he needed exercise to keep his body strong.

Colleges in those days had no football teams. They had no baseball teams, no track squads. Tom liked to run, though, just for the fun of running.

At the end of every mile along the road leading into Williamsburg there was a big stone, to show people driving into town how much farther they had to go. The first of these stones was just one mile from town.

"I'll run out to the first milestone and back," thought Tom. "That ought to give me exercise enough. Then I can start studying again."

He ran down the steps, across the college grounds and down the main street.

A big coach was clattering over the stones. It was drawn by six horses. Inside sat the governor of Virginia. He called to his coachman to stop. The governor and Tom talked several minutes.

"Don't forget," the governor said, as he started on again, "that you are going to have dinner with me tomorrow."

There was no danger of Tom's forgetting. Dinner at the governor's Palace would be quite different from dinner at the college, where the food was good, but plain.

Even more than the dinner, though, Tom liked the company at the governor's. There would probably be only four of them there, and Tom would be the only young man. He would do very little of the talking. He would just sit back and listen. Tom was a good talker, but his professor was right—he was a good listener, too. He enjoyed one just as much as he did the other.

He stood for a moment watching the governor's coach drive away. He watched the great gates to the Palace open. It was good to know that they would be opening for him tomorrow.

He turned back to the road before him, thinking, "If I am going out to dinner tomorrow there is a lot of studying that I ought to finish tonight. I had better be moving along."

He started running again, on out to the milepost and back.

"HELLO, EB!"

On his way back he passed Raleigh Tavern. A stranger was getting down from his horse there. As Tom passed, the servant held his lantern so that Tom saw the stranger's face.

"Eb!" cried Tom.

Eb turned. He was certainly glad to see Tom.

Tom was glad to see his friend. "What are you doing here, Eb?"

"Mr. Maury sent me down with some papers for his lawyer."

Tom could see that Eb was indeed very proud that Mr. Maury had chosen to send him on such an important errand.

"Come right on up to my room, Eb, and tell me all about it."

"I must finish Mr. Maury's business tonight. If I could come tomorrow morning——"

"Of course," said Tom.

He was studying the next morning when Eb knocked at his door.

"Come in," he called.

Eb came in.

"My!" said Tom. "It's good to see you. You haven't changed a bit."

Eb looked around the room. It was such a nice room, it made him feel awkward. He was used to a log cabin with a bare floor, and home-made stools and tables. All this fine carpet and

162

furniture, and Tom's fine clothes made him feel very uncomfortable. As soon as Tom began to talk, though, everything was all right again. Tom hadn't changed a bit either.

"Tell me all about the folks back home," Tom said. "And tell me about the mountains. Are the peach trees blooming yet? Tell me all about you and your grandfather."

They were still talking when Dabney and another friend came in.

"Have you forgotten you were going to dinner at the governor's?" asked Dabney. "You'd better hurry."

"Of course I hadn't forgotten," said Tom. "The time has just been going too fast for me to keep up. That's all."

He fastened the silver buckles at his knees. He picked up his cocked hat.

"Come on, Eb. We can walk as far as the Palace garden together."

They started down the steps. Dabney's friend laughed.

"If that isn't exactly like Tom!" he said. "He is busy visiting with an ignorant fellow from the backwoods one minute and off to dinner with the governor the next!'"

"Of course it's like Tom," said Dabney. "He's friendly with everybody."

Back to the Little Mountain

Two YOUNG men were climbing the little mountain. They had started early in the morning, before the sun was hot. They had brought books with them. Liza Ann had packed a tempting lunch for them. They had paddled across the river in Tom's canoe.

Tom had graduated from William and Mary College. He was home now for a visit. Dabney Carr had come along with him. Of all the sights at Shadwell, the one Tom wanted most of all to show Dabney was his little mountain.

Up and up they climbed and, every minute as they climbed, they talked.

Most of the men in Virginia were talking about the same thing now, and asking the same questions. Did King George have the right to tell the people in America what taxes they must pay, instead of letting them decide it for themselves? Must the people in America obey laws made in England? Must they obey laws which they had had no share in making?

"All people," said Tom, "are born equal. We have the right to make our own laws and govern ourselves. We ought to be free."

"That is an easy thing to say," Dabney told him, "but liberty isn't an easy thing to get, and it isn't an easy thing to keep."

"I know," said Tom. "It's like climbing this mountain. There is nothing easy about it, but it is worth it."

The little mountain grew steeper now. They couldn't talk and climb at the same time. Their faces grew red and their breath began to come in little gasps. The briars caught at them and held them back. The low branches of trees brushed their faces.

"It is a stiff climb," said Dabney. "I shall be glad when we can stop and rest. Won't you?"

"Yes," said Tom.

Then, all at once, they were at the top. The sun was shining. There was a cool breeze blowing from the west.

Toward the east there were no hills. The boys could see for miles and miles around until, at last, the earth and sky seemed to come together in a faraway line across the horizon.

Toward the west there were the Blue Mountains and beyond them were thousands of miles of mountains and plains and rivers. There were lands no white man had ever seen.

"It is a wonderful country!" said Dabney.

"It must be a free country," said Tom.

They sat down beneath a big oak tree to rest.

Soon they opened their lunchbox and ate golden fried chicken, boiled eggs, and cold cornbread.

"I wonder," said Tom, "what it will all be like two hundred years from now."

Dabney laughed. "There is one thing certain —*we* won't be here to see."

"No," Tom agreed, "but maybe some of our ideas will still be here. You know, Dabney, sometimes ideas are bigger things than men."

A Law Student
Listens

AFTER TOM graduated from the College of William and Mary he began to study law. Part of the time he could stay at Shadwell, with his books. Often, though, he had to go to Williamsburg, where Mr. Wythe lived. He was the lawyer under whom Tom was studying. Tom always asked many questions. Mr. Wythe asked questions, too, and suggested what to study next.

The road to Williamsburg was a lonesome one. It led through deep dark forests and alongside great fields of tobacco and corn. The trip was a long one, but Tom liked it that way—it gave him plenty of time to think.

He had plenty to think about, goodness knew! There were the dances going on in town. There was the new home he wanted to build. Most of all, there were the questions he and Dabney had been talking about. Tom felt that the time was coming very soon when he must speak up for that which he believed. First, though, he wanted to be very sure, himself.

PATRICK HENRY IS SPEAKING

The morning after he reached Williamsburg, he started out for Lawyer Wythe's office. On the way he passed several of his friends. They all seemed to be quite excited about something.

"What's up?" asked Tom.

"We're having a big argument. Join in, if you want to."

"No, thanks."

"Why not?"

170

"I don't like arguments."

"For goodness' sake, why?"

"If I am better at it than you are, it isn't fair to you. If you are better than I am, then it's not fair to me."

"Suppose we are both of us good?"

"I knew two men like that once. Each one was so good he convinced the other. They had to start arguing all over again, because each one now was on the opposite side from where he had started!"

"Look here, Tom. If you don't ever argue with folks, how do you always manage to make them think as you do?"

"I don't."

"Most of the time you do. How?"

Tom thought for a minute. Then he grinned. "I always try to be polite, for one thing. Sometimes, maybe, I ask a question or two to set the other fellow to thinking. 'Don't you think?' 'I wonder if——' You know—things like that.

Pretty soon he is figuring things out for himself. That is what I am after. Now he doesn't think of it any longer as being *my* idea. It is *his* idea.

"Folks always like their own ideas. He begins to feel that I am agreeing with him, not he with me. That's all right. I don't mind. We are agreeing. That is the important thing."

"I know a man who is as good at all that as you are."

"I know one who is ever so much better."

"Who?"

"Mr. Patrick Henry."

"He is the one I am talking about. He is just about the finest speaker I ever heard. He is from the backwoods, like yourself, isn't he, Tom?"

"Not quite so far back, but pretty close."

"He has a golden tongue, all right. Say, someone told me he might be speaking at the House of Burgesses today. Let's go see."

Patrick Henry hadn't forgotten that he was

going to look Tom up. More than once, when he came to Williamsburg, he had knocked on the door of Tom's little room. In no time at all they would be telling each other jokes. Patrick Henry called it "spinning yarns."

After a while they would become serious. "How do you stand on this tax question, Tom?" Mr. Henry asked. "Do you think we should just go ahead and pay whatever England tells us to?"

"No," said Tom, "I don't." He thought for a minute. He never liked to use long words when short ones would do just as well. Sometimes, though, long ones were really better. "It is taxation without representation."

"Exactly. That is just what this Stamp Act is. England wants to *make* us buy tax stamps to put on our newspapers and cards and almanacs and ever so many other things. Well, we are not going to do it—not if I can get people to feel the way I do about it."

Later, on the way to the meeting hall, Tom met several of his friends.

"I wonder what Mr. Henry will talk about?" one young man said as they hurried along.

Tom remembered that last conversation. "I expect it will be the Stamp Act. That is what everyone is excited about."

TOM BECOMES SURE

The hall where the Burgesses were meeting was packed. The boys couldn't get in any further than the doorway. That was far enough for Tom. He was so tall he could see over the heads of the crowd. Patrick Henry's voice could be heard in every corner of the room.

Yes, he was talking about the Stamp Act. It was a famous speech he made that day. Copies of it were sent to New York, to Massachusetts, to Pennsylvania, and all of the other colonies in

America. In every colony the people began to get together. "We shall *not* pay the Stamp Tax. We shall *not* have taxation without representation."

Tom didn't make up his mind in a hurry. There had been his talks with Dabney. There had been his thoughts during the long ride to Williamsburg. Patrick Henry's speech was the final touch. Now at last he was sure. The American colonies must govern themselves. They must be free.

Monticello

Tom HAD become a man now. He had a man's work to do. He became a lawyer—a very good one. It wasn't long before people were saying, "Young Jefferson knows law. He can help you."

He had just left the courthouse one afternoon. He stopped to chat with some friends.

"Look!" said one of them. "Isn't that Caesar coming down the road?"

"It can't be. I left him back at Shadwell."

It was Caesar, though. He looked as if he had come a long way in a hurry. His clothes were covered with mud. So was his horse.

"Something has happened." Tom's heart was in

his mouth. "Caesar!" he called. "Here I am! Is everyone at Shadwell all right?"

"Yes sir—only there isn't any Shadwell any more. It's burned to the ground."

Caesar climbed down from his horse. He reached in his pocket for a letter. "Your sister has written you all about it."

The young man was so excited he couldn't wait for Mister Tom to read the letter. He went on telling about it himself. "The whole house is gone. All the furniture is burned up and all your clothes except what you've got with you. Everything got burned to ashes."

"Was anybody hurt?"

"Not a soul. We managed to get all the folks out of the house, but that was all we could do. It looked like those flames were so hungry they licked up everything they could reach—the silver teapot and the spoons and everything. Yes, Mister Tom—everything's gone."

His sister's letter said the same thing. Tom could hardly believe it.

"My books?" He had spent a lot of money on his books, but that wasn't the only reason they meant so much to him. He had read them many times. "Weren't any of them saved?"

"Not a single one," Caesar said.

"And my papers?" There were all of his notebooks filled with his outlines of the books he had read. There were his notes on the cases he was to take to court next month. He had spent hours and hours working over them.

"Not a scrap of paper was left." Then Caesar grinned. "Don't you fret. Everything is all right. We saved your fiddle."

NEW IDEAS

Tom didn't have much time to play his fiddle now. He had to build himself a new home. He had started it before the fire but now he had to hurry to complete it.

He was building it right where the boys had said he would—on top of his little mountain. The Italian word for "little mountain" is Monticello. It made a fine name for his beautiful home.

Monticello was as fine as its name. He loved it and worked on it until it became one of the loveliest homes in all the American colonies. It wasn't only the house that was beautiful. It was filled with beautiful things.

Even that wasn't enough. He wanted all of his beautiful things to be useful. Now he had a chance to try out all the inventions and new ideas the boys back at school had teased him about. Some of these ideas didn't work. Many did.

He made a big clock for his hall. It had two faces. One was on the inside. The other was out on the porch. The clock was so high up on the wall that he needed a ladder when he wound it.

That didn't bother Tom. He invented a ladder which, when it wasn't being used, folded up in such a manner that it looked like a long pole.

He invented double doors which could be opened at the same time with one touch. He invented a writing desk big enough to use at home, but which could be folded so it was small enough for him to use when he traveled.

He had as many ideas for inventions for the farm as he did for the inside of his house. He invented a new plow, which was so useful that it was copied all over the United States and Europe.

All through his long life, whenever he traveled in either the United States or Europe, he was always looking for new plants and seeds. He brought them back to try on his farm.

On New Year's Day of 1772, Tom, now twenty-nine years old, married Martha Skelton, a beautiful and talented young widow. They spent ten happy years together at Monticello.

Of their six children, Martha and Mary grew to womanhood and were Tom's especial pride.

THE NATURAL BRIDGE

Just before the Revolutionary War Tom made a trip far back into the mountains. At last he saw the Giant's Bridge Eb's granddad had told him about. It was every bit as beautiful as the old man had said. To look at it made a person feel small, but it rested and inspired him, too.

Tom decided he would like to have this natural bridge for his own. The King of England still claimed all of the lands in this back country. His agents sold Tom the natural bridge and the land around it.

As soon as he owned it, Tom wanted to share it. He built a small house close by the bridge so that travelers could have a shelter when they came to see this wonder of the world.

The Declaration of Independence

JOURNEYS WERE interesting but Tom didn't want them to last too long. He was always anxious to get back home to his little mountain. Each year, though, he had less time to spend there. When he was a boy he had listened to the men who governed Virginia. Now he was one of them. Soon he would be leading them.

In 1775 there was a convention in Richmond. Tom was one of the men elected to attend it. The convention was held in St. John's Church. The church was small. It looked quiet and peaceful. It wasn't a quiet and peaceful convention.

King George still refused to let the people of

Virginia govern themselves. He refused to let them have any share in deciding what taxes they must pay. What would Virginia do about it?

The King had sent his soldiers to fight the people of Massachusetts. What was Virginia going to do about that? Should she help the King? Should she help her friends in Massachusetts? Maybe the King was sending soldiers to fight against Virginia, too. What was Virginia going to do about that?

Everyone was excited. Some people said that Virginia should do one thing. Some said another.

Then Patrick Henry began to speak. The people grew quiet. Everyone leaned forward to listen. Those outside crowded close to the windows. Tom could feel the excitement like waves all around him.

"I know not what course others may take," cried Patrick Henry, as he finished his speech, "but, as for me, give me liberty or give me death!"

He had answered the questions everyone was asking. Virginia must be free.

Then and there plans began to be made. Thomas Jefferson was one of the men chosen to help make them.

WRITING THE DECLARATION

It was one thing to say that the American Colonies must be free. It was another to make them so. Certainly one of the first steps was to get them to act together.

That was why, in 1776, men from all of the colonies gathered together in Philadelphia for a Continental Congress. Tom had to leave his little mountain again.

It was a long hard trip from Monticello to Williamsburg. To Philadelphia, it was harder and longer still. His little gig was hardly more than a chair with two big wheels. It took only one horse to pull it. The horse had a hard time when it came to the mudholes in the road or rocks so big they almost turned both Tom and his carriage over.

He was tired when he reached Philadelphia. The weather was hot. He felt sticky and dirty. He had no time, though, to think about these things. He found two rooms where he could sleep and work and talk to his friends.

As soon as they knew he had arrived, they came hurrying to see him. "It is high time you were here," they said. "There is much work for you to do."

They knew that Tom wasn't too good at making speeches. His voice didn't carry too well. He didn't like to argue. But how he could write! His sentences were as clear and straight as his thoughts. He never used two words where one would do. Everyone who could read could understand exactly what he meant.

His friends were right. There was work for him to do. He was the next to the youngest man in Congress, but he was quickly put on a committee to write a Declaration of Independence.

There were five men on the committee. Benjamin Franklin was one of them. John Adams was another. They met and discussed what they wanted to say. Then they asked Tom to do the actual writing.

Tom went to work at once. Day after hot day he kept at it. Night after night he was still at work. Flies and bugs buzzed around his candle. He used one handkerchief after another to wipe his moist face.

He had no books—he didn't need them. He had been reading and making notes ever since he was a boy. His mind and his memory were well trained. He knew what the people of America wanted to say. His task was to find the best way to say it.

At last the work was finished. He made a fair copy. The committee studied it carefully. They made a few changes. Then it was taken to the Congress.

Tom's actual work was finished, but the worst part was still to come. He had to sit there while his Declaration was torn to pieces. It was taken up sentence by sentence. "Leave this out." "Change this." "Put this in."

Tom didn't try to argue. He didn't become angry. He sat quietly. Sometimes, though, his friends could see him wince.

The meetings were being held in Independence Hall. There was a stable close by. Horseflies from the stable buzzed in through the open windows. The men slapped at the pesky things. The debate went on.

Finally a vote was taken. Only a few words of Tom's were changed. A few sentences were left out. Then the Declaration of Independence was passed. Congress had declared that the people of America were a free people.

HIS MOST IMPORTANT WORK

Tom was still a young man. He had a long and busy life ahead of him. He became governor of Virginia. He went to France to make friends for America. He became vice-president and then president of the new United States of America.

Even with all his work and cares he never forgot boys like Eb. He knew they needed the chance which only an education could give them. He made plans for free education in Virginia. When he was older, he started a college for the young men of his state. It was only five miles from Monticello. From there he could watch through his telescope while it was being built.

What was his most important work? He, himself, listed three things:

1. The Declaration of Independence.

2. The law which gave each person the right to worship God in his own way.

3. The University of Virginia.

Some people would change this list. Some would add one thing, some another. On one point they all agreed. Thomas Jefferson was one of the greatest leaders that America has ever known.